Five-Minute Bedtime Tales

This edition published in 2002 by Dean, an imprint of Egmont Books Limited,
239 Kensington High Street, London W8 6SA

First published as three separate books by Dean:
5-Minute Dinosaur Tales for Bedtime Copyright © 1994 Egmont Books Limited
5-Minute Farmyard Tales for Bedtime Copyright © 1995 Egmont Books Limited
5-Minute Jungle Tales for Bedtime Copyright © 1995 Egmont Books Limited

This combined edition Copyright © 2002 by Egmont Books Limited

Printed and bound in U.A.E

Five-Minute
Bedtime Tales

Illustrated by
Peter Stevenson

DEAN

Felicity the foal was fed up with all the other animals in the farmyard teasing her.

'You've got such long, wobbly legs,' they laughed, 'you'll never be able to enter the roller skating race at school.'

Her mother bought her two lovely pairs of red skates – one pair for her front legs and one for the back. Felicity was very proud of them, but every time she tried to move along her legs got in a tangle and she fell over.

'Keep on practising,' her father said from over the stable door. 'You'll get the hang of it in the end.'

The day of the race arrived. The headmaster, Mr Cockerel, lifted the starting flag and they were off. Felicity was a little slow at first, but gradually her long legs took her past the leader and she skated home the winner.

'See,' she cried, 'long legs can be useful sometimes. Perhaps I'll be a racehorse one day!'

Farmer Robin hung his favourite old felt hat on a nail in the barn. He had worn it every winter for years. During the springtime, he hung it on the nail and only wore it on rainy days.

'I ought to throw it away and buy myself a new one,' he said to himself, looking at the battered old hat. 'But I'll keep it just in case.'

As the days became warmer, Mr and Mrs Robin began to look for a nesting site.

'This is just the place,' Mrs Robin said excitedly when she found the old hat. Soon they had built a nest of twigs and lined it with soft feathers and sheeps' wool which had caught on the fences. Mrs Robin laid six pale green eggs and proudly brooded over them.

Once the eggs hatched, the robins were very busy. They flew in and out of the barn, bringing food to their hungry family.

Then one rainy day, Farmer Robin came to fetch his old hat.

'Well, bless my soul,' he smiled. 'That old hat hasn't outlived its usefulness after all.' And he left the hat where it was for the robins to nest in every spring.

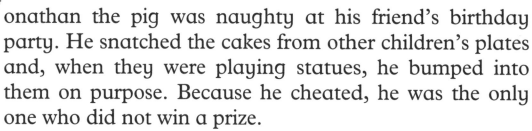

Jonathan the pig was naughty at his friend's birthday party. He snatched the cakes from other children's plates and, when they were playing statues, he bumped into them on purpose. Because he cheated, he was the only one who did not win a prize.

When the party was over, all the children were given a balloon. Jonathan's was a big shiny red one.

'I want a blue one,' he yelled, stamping his foot.

Caroline was holding a blue balloon. Jonathan chased after her, grabbed the balloon and ran off. The balloon flew behind him in the wind. Jonathan turned into a field. Faster and faster he ran. It was fun!

But then Jonathan tripped and fell. He let go of the balloon and it floated up into the sky. The wind carried the balloon along fast, until suddenly it stopped blowing. The balloon began to sink down.

Oh dear! It rested on top of a blackberry bush. Jonathan climbed carefully into the prickly bush to reach the balloon. Just as he took hold of the string – POP! The balloon burst. Jonathan licked his scratches and set off home empty-handed.

'Mum always said naughty pigs end up with nothing,' he said sadly. 'She was right.'

The ducks watched the dark green mallard fly down and land on their pond. They stayed among the reeds, but Mary Moorhen liked to chat to visitors. She was proud of their pond. It had water lilies and it was ever so big. It pleased her when other birds admitted that their ponds were not nearly as large or beautiful.

'Hello, I'm Mary,' she chirped. 'Welcome to our wonderful, big pond. Where are you from?'

'I'm Chuck,' he said, 'and I have just flown here from Canada across the most splendid, huge pond.'

Mary was not happy to hear this. She swam round in a little circle, making ripples on the pond.

'Is that pond wider than this?' she asked.

The drake laughed and stuck his tail in the air.

'Of course,' he replied. 'Much wider.'

She pointed with her beak at the far reeds.

'Is it longer than that?' Again the drake laughed.

'It is much longer.' She pointed at the farm buildings on a distant bank.

'Surely it cannot be bigger than this?' she said.

'Silly thing,' said Chuck. 'I have flown over the Atlantic Ocean. It is so big that when you look at it, you can see no end and no beginning.' For once, it was Mary's turn to be impressed, and she wondered whether she would ever see that splendid, huge pond.

Toby the tom cat was a typical farm cat. He had typically long claws and typically sharp white teeth that shone when he smiled. He swaggered across the farmyard by day, flexing his typically large tom cat muscles. All the birds and mice in the farmyard were frightened of him. He looked very fierce indeed.

But Toby wasn't really typical at all. In fact, Toby had a very unusual secret. Next time you visit the farmyard at night, when all the other animals are asleep, and you are very quiet, you might just hear a rather odd sound that goes TIPPETY TAP TAP.

For when night falls, Toby the typical tom cat likes to tap dance. Now that isn't typical at all, is it?

Bernard the chick was bigger than all the other chicks. He was also greedier and bossier. In fact, when they were really fed up with him, the other chicks used to call him Big Bossy Bernard.

At mealtimes, when the farmer's wife scattered the corn, Bernard would gobble up as much as he could, pushing the others out of the way and saying, 'I'm bigger than you! I need more food.'

One day he found a trail of corn running across the yard from a tiny hole in the farmer's wife's basket.

'I can have this all to myself!' he said. Greedily he ate the trail of corn, not paying attention to where he was going. Suddenly – BUMP! Bernard was knocked to the ground and peered up to see a great big goose looking at him crossly.

'Keep away from my corn,' the bird hissed, pecking at him with its sharp beak. 'I'm bigger than you! I need more food.'

Bernard did not wait to argue. He was off across the farmyard as fast as his little legs could carry him. And after that, he felt a lot less 'big' and he was certainly a lot less 'bossy'!

Samson the puppy couldn't wait for the end of term. 'School's so boring,' he said to his mother. 'I shall have two whole weeks off at Easter. I'll play all day long, from the minute I wake up until the minute I go to bed. It'll be smashing.'

So on the last day of term he came bounding back from school, his lunch box on his back.

'I'm home, Mum,' he called. 'Now I'm really ready to have some fun.'

On the first morning of the holidays he chased the ducks and chickens, and swam in the stream in the afternoon. On the second day he followed the farmer's wife down to the village to do her shopping, and on the third day he watched the farmer haymaking. But by the fourth day he was feeling a bit lonely – and *very* bored.

'When does school start again, Mum?' he said. 'It's so boring at home. I can't wait for the beginning of term to see my friends again!'

P at the cat liked living on the farm. Today she was especially happy, for her kittens were on their first outing. She led them out of the barn and into the sunlight. They looked around – timid but excited! Then they began to explore, staying close to their mum.

Joe was the bravest and wandered a little further away. He saw Rachael Duck waddle past, followed by a trail of ducklings. They were little, fuzzy and brown – just like him. Joe thought they were another cat family.

'I'll follow them,' he thought, joining the queue. 'This is good fun,' he said, although he did find it rather hard to waddle like the ducklings.

When they came to the pond, Rachael hopped straight into the water, followed by her little ones. Joe followed them bravely. But he didn't float like they did and the water felt horrible! He jumped out and shook himself dry.

Just then he saw some little, fuzzy brown creatures playing in the yard. He looked at them. Then he looked at the ducklings. They were very similar – but they weren't the same! He rushed back to the safety of his mum. He would never make that mistake again!

It was a hot day on the farm, so the animals decided to have a Fun Day.

Timmy Too Slow, the tortoise, got his name by being too slow at whatever he did.

Timmy entered the first race, but by the time he started to move forward, Rex had already won.

'Ha, ha, ha, Timmy, you are just too slow,' the animals laughed.

At the three-legged race no-one wanted to be Timmy's partner because they thought he would never win. He was awful at the egg and spoon race, and even worse at the sack race because he could not jump.

Mrs. Cluck announced that the last game would be statues and if anyone moved, even a little bit, they would be out.

Everyone tried to stand perfectly still, but they all dropped out, until only Timmy was left. He was just 'too slow'.

Mrs Potawick was always grumpy. When it was hot, she complained of sunburn. When it was cold, she wanted the sun to shine. If the pigsty was muddy, she wanted it clean. If it was clean, she wanted to roll in the mud.

'Hello, Mrs Potawick,' said Matt the sheepdog one day. 'Lovely weather today.'

'It's far too hot,' grumbled grumpy Mrs Potawick.

'You've got nothing to grumble about,' replied Matt. 'I have to chase sheep all day.'

Wilma the cow walked past on her way to milking.

'Hello, Mrs Potawick. How are you today?'

'I'm tired and I've got a sore foot,' she grumbled.

'You've got nothing to grumble about,' replied Wilma. 'The farmer is late with milking, I've walked all the way from the top field and my udder is full.'

Later that day, Farmer Brown came and cleaned out the pigsty, leaving just a little mud in the corner. He washed Mrs Potawick and gave her a good scratch in her favourite spot. He filled up one trough with food and the other with fresh water. Matt and Wilma passed the sty, expecting to hear her usual grumbles.

'Hello, Mrs Potawick,' they said. 'Feeling better?' Mrs Potawick opened her mouth to speak. But she could not think of a single thing to grumble about!

Bobby the kid's dad could fix anything. Mr Goat could fix clocks, radios, bicycles, you name it, he could fix it.

One day, Bobby was out playing with a big red balloon when the balloon landed on a rosebush thorn and burst. Bobby wasn't sad though – he knew his dad could fix it. He could fix anything.

'I'm afraid I can't fix it this time,' said his dad, sadly. 'Some things just can't be fixed.' Bobby began to cry, but suddenly Mr Goat said, 'I know what I *can* fix though – your sad face, young Bobby.' And with that, Mr Goat gave Bobby a brand new red balloon and a big kiss.

Bobby was happy again – perhaps his dad could fix everything after all.

Jeffrey the pony had an old bicycle which needed painting. The trouble was that Jeffrey could not decide which colour to paint it.

'Paint it green,' said Sybil the sheep. 'Grass is green and that's my favourite food.'

'No, no, no,' said Philip Pig. 'Pink is best – pigs are pink so pink must be the best colour.'

'Blue!' cried Mr Duck, 'like the colour of my pond.'

'It must be yellow,' argued Gertrude the chick. 'Like my lovely soft feathers.'

No-one could agree, and Jeffrey was very confused. Suddenly, he had an idea and off he went with his paintbrush, without a word to anyone.

What a surprise when Jeffrey returned to show off his newly painted bicycle. Its handlebars were green, the pedals were pink, the seat was blue and the wheels were bright yellow.

Now everyone was happy!

Mrs Turkey was calling her chicks.

'Gobble, gobble,' she said . 'It's bedtime.'

But Tilly Turkey wouldn't listen. She just carried on playing in the farmyard.

Mrs Turkey held out her wing, and all the other chicks scrambled underneath. It was cosy and warm, and they were soon asleep. But Tilly Turkey just kept on playing.

All of a sudden, there was a rumble of thunder. Then came a flash of lightning. The rain began to pour down.

Tilly Turkey ran and hid beneath her mother's wing. All the other chicks were warm and dry, but Tilly was cold and wet. She woke them up.

They were so annoyed that they pushed her out into the rain again.

'Let me in,' begged Tilly Turkey.

Mrs Turkey felt sorry for Tilly. She lifted up her other wing so that Tilly could come in out of the rain.

'If you are lonely and wet, it's all your own fault,' said Mrs Turkey.

But Tilly didn't hear her. She was already fast asleep!

One day four new cows arrived at the farm. Buttercup, the oldest cow, welcomed them and asked them their names.

'Daisy,' answered the first cow.

'Daisy,' answered the second cow.

'Daisy,' answered the third cow.

'Good heavens!' cried Buttercup. 'Three of you all called Daisy! How very extraordinary. We'll have to call you Daisy One, Daisy Two, and Daisy Three!' She turned to the fourth cow. 'Are you called Daisy, too?' she asked.

'Certainly not,' said the cow with her nose in the air. 'Daisy is a very *ordinary* name, and I am a very extraordinary cow. My name is Eglantine.' And she walked away to the other end of the field.

What Eglantine did not realize, however, was that at that end of the field it was very muddy. One minute she was happily chewing clover – and the next she was stuck in the mud! Desperately she mooed for help.

'Quick!' said Buttercup, and the Daisies *were* quick. Daisy One caught hold of Eglantine by the tail, Daisy Two grabbed Daisy One by the tail, and Daisy Three grabbed Daisy Two by the tail. Together they pulled Eglantine out of the mud.

'Thank you!' said the frightened cow. 'I'll never look down on the Daisies again. After all, I was rescued by a Daisy chain!'

Penny Pig's sty was the envy of all the other farmyard animals. It was warm and cosy and painted a lovely bright blue. But Penny still wasn't happy with her home. She wanted a view!

'It's no problem for you,' she said to Hank, the cart horse. 'You're so big and tall you can see for miles from your stable door.'

Hank thought hard about what Penny had said. He decided to surprise her with a solution to her problem.

The next day while she was out in the fields, he found a small wooden chair that had been left in the barn. He fixed it to the roof of Penny's sty. Next, he nailed an old piece of fencing to the sty to make a ladder.

When Penny came back she was thrilled! Sitting in the chair on top of her home she could see over the whole farm. She had a view at last!

Tommy Toad lived in a pond at the bottom of the farm.

'I wish I were not so ugly,' moaned Tommy. 'I am brown and crinkly and covered in bumps.' He looked at his reflection in the green pond water and a large, wet tear slid down his crinkly brown cheek.

'No one will ever love me,' he cried one day, as he swam sadly to the bottom of the pond and hid under a weed.

Lucy and her brother Tim were fishing in the pond. Tim caught Tommy in the bottom of his net.

'Look at this,' said Tim. Lucy looked in the net.

'Ugh!' she said. 'What a horrible, brown, crinkly thing.' Tommy jumped out of the net.

'No one loves me,' he croaked. 'I am so ugly!'

But as he sank through the water he passed . . . another toad. She was brown and crinkly and covered in bumps.

'Hello,' Tommy said. 'I have not met you before.'

'I am new to the pond,' she said. 'My name is Priscilla.' Tommy's heart began to thump.

'I'm Tommy,' he gasped. 'And I think you're lovely.' Priscilla blushed.

'Thank you,' she said shyly. 'You are the most handsome toad that I have ever seen.' And they hopped off happily – the best looking pair of toads in the pond.

The most exciting part of the day on Acorn Farm was when Mr Duck the postman delivered the early morning letters.

Every morning, Glenda the donkey would trot down to the gate with the other animals to meet him.

'Is there a letter for me?' asked Glenda, hopefully.

'Sorry, not today,' Mr Duck would reply.

Day after day went by and poor Glenda never ever got a letter.

In the end, Glenda didn't even bother to ask – she knew there would be no letters for her. She just watched from her field sadly as the other animals collected their postcards and parcels.

One day, Mr Duck suddenly shouted, 'Hey Glenda! Don't you want your letter?'

Glenda's heart missed a beat. 'For me?' she cried.

'Yes. All the way from Australia,' said Mr Duck.

Glenda tore open her letter. 'It's from my sister!' she shouted. 'She's coming to visit!'

And Glenda was even more proud when the animals all agreed that her letter was indeed the best letter ever.

Pamela Pig lay on her back in the pigsty. She rolled over and over in the mud. She loved mud. Cuthbert Calf popped his head over the wall.

'Don't forget the picnic,' he said. But Pamela just grunted. She knew her mum would make her clean herself up first and she couldn't be bothered.

'It's time to get ready, Pamela,' said Gertie Goat.

'Baa-baa,' bleated Lennie Lamb. 'Picnic time!'

Pamela took no notice. She rubbed some mud on her tummy. She shook herself so it made lovely gloopy sounds. She would rather have fun being muddy than go to a picnic.

The farmyard grew quiet. Pamela's tummy rumbled. She thought of the others eating all the lovely picnic food. How she wished she had got ready in time!

A few raindrops splashed down, then more and more.

'I'm in luck!' Pamela shouted. The rain quickly washed away the mud. Soon Pamela was pink all over, from the tip of her pointed ears to the end of her curly tail. She waddled to the barn where the others were sheltering. Then the rain stopped and the sun came out.

'Come on!' Pamela cried. 'Let's eat. I'm starving.' They carried the baskets of food into the field and they all enjoyed a wonderful picnic.

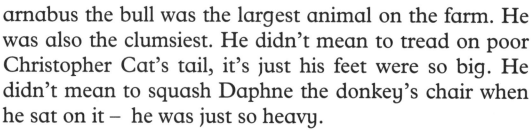

Barnabus the bull was the largest animal on the farm. He was also the clumsiest. He didn't mean to tread on poor Christopher Cat's tail, it's just his feet were so big. He didn't mean to squash Daphne the donkey's chair when he sat on it – he was just so heavy.

One day while walking along day-dreaming, clumsy old Barnabus bumped into Mrs Hen's apple tree.

'Oh no!' cried Barnabus. 'I've knocked all the apples off Mrs Hen's tree. Whatever shall I do?'

Barnabus was just thinking he might be able to glue the apples back on the tree when Mrs Hen came hurrying out of the hen house.

'Oh thank you so much for picking all the apples, Barnabus. I was too small to reach them,' she said. And Mrs Hen baked Barnabus a huge apple pie that night as a reward.

Beryl Bee had been busy all day gathering honey from the flowers. Without noticing, she had wandered far from home. Beryl Bee was lost.

'Where am I?' asked Beryl. Looking around, all she could see were flowers.

Just then Chirpy Chicken came hopping by.

'I didn't know you lived on the farm,' said Chirpy.

'I live in a beehive in the orchard,' said Beryl, 'but I can't find my way back.'

'I'll show you the way home,' said Chirpy Chicken.

Beryl Bee buzzed along behind Chirpy Chicken, and soon they reached the beehive. But a stray dog started to bark at Chirpy.

'I'm scared,' said Chirpy.

'I'm not,' said Beryl.

She buzzed around the dog's ears and settled on his nose. He had been stung once when he was a puppy, and didn't like it. The dog stopped barking and ran off.

'Thank you for rescuing me,' said Chirpy Chicken.

'One good turn deserves another,' said Beryl Bee. 'Thank you for leading me back to the beehive. Won't you stay to tea? I've got lots of delicious honey.'

How could he refuse?

atilda was a tiny, furry kitten with cute pink ears and claws like needles. Each time little Susie tried to stroke her, she scratched her and spat.

One day, Matilda escaped from her basket and went to explore, looking for somebody to scratch.

First she met the carthorse. His feet were too big and hairy to scratch, so Matilda went on. The cows had fierce horns, so she avoided them. Next she saw ducks and hens who all had hard, snapping beaks, so she didn't try to frighten them either.

At last she found a creature who was even smaller than herself – a little mouse.

'Hello,' said the mouse. 'Are you new here?'

Matilda pushed out her claws and tried to look fierce.

'You poor little thing,' said the mouse, kindly. 'Don't be frightened. Have you lost your mummy?'

Matilda felt very silly, so she sat down and pretended to wash her face. Suddenly, she heard a loud 'Mee-ow!' She looked up and there, towering over her, was an enormous striped tiger. Matilda was terrified.

Just then, Susie appeared and shooed the tiger away. 'Naughty kitty,' said Susie. 'Come home. The big farm cats here are too fierce for a tiny kitten like you!'

Matilda curled up in Susie's arms and purred with relief. And she never spat or scratched Susie again.

Hunker was a huge, bouncy puppy with enormous padded paws and a long tail which he wagged so hard that it sometimes knocked the farmer's two little boys right over. Timmy and Tommy did not mind a bit. They loved him, and often went to sleep in his basket with their heads on his tummy.

Their mother would see them and smile.

'People think Hunker's fierce because he is so huge. But just look at that softy!' she said.

One day a bad fox came to the farm to steal a chicken. Hunker bounded up to say 'Hello,' wagging his tail so hard that it knocked the fox to the ground. He stood over the frightened fox, grinning his puppy grin.

'Dad!' shouted Timmy. 'Look, brave Hunker's caught a thief!'

'Keep still, or Hunker will eat you!' said Tommy, knowing perfectly well that Hunker was only playing. The farmer came and patted Hunker.

'Good pup!' he said. 'You'll soon be a fine guard dog. Get up, you naughty fox! Hunker won't hurt you. But never take what doesn't belong to you again.'

Mrs Patsy Pig's young family had eaten their breakfast and were snoozing in the sty. It was midsummer and very hot.

'I'm going out for an hour to see an old friend,' she said. 'Mind you stay in the shade. Your skin is very pink and you're not very hairy, so you could get sunburnt.'

As soon as she was out of sight, Percy, the largest and naughtiest of the eight piglets, scampered over to the patch of sunlight in the middle of the sty.

'Come on,' he called to the others. 'It's lovely and warm here.'

Soon all the piglets were having a super time chasing each other from the sun into the shade and back again. It was a very tiring game, and one by one they fell asleep – in the sun!

When Mrs Pig arrived home she found eight very sore piglets. 'I told you to stay out of the sun, didn't I?' she scolded. 'I hope you've learned your lesson!'

I shall be sorry to see this old thing go,' said Farmer William, looking rather sadly at his old tractor as it stood at the side of the yard. 'But it is just too old to be repaired any more. It will have to stay here until the scrap man can come and take it away.'

Madeleine the donkey overheard all this and it made her sad. The old tractor had rescued Isobel the cow from the bog. Bella the dog just loved to ride on the back behind the farmer, and the sheep watched for it on the coldest winter days when the farmer brought them extra hay for food. So she gathered all the animals together and they decided what they would do.

'I need somewhere safe to have my kittens,' said Snowball. 'I'll make a nest under the big wheels.'

'I need a nest too,' piped up Robin. 'I'll build it under the seat.'

'I can stretch out on the bonnet when I sunbathe in the morning,' added Primrose Cat.

'And I can curl up on the floor when I'm worn out from rounding up the sheep,' put in Bella.

Farmer William soon realised that he would not be able to move the old tractor even if he wanted to. But he was really rather glad!

Danny Duckling was gliding on the water in the duck pond when he noticed a strange, green creature swimming by.

'What a funny fish,' Danny thought. He hurried off to tell his brother and sister, Derek and Dinah, what he had just seen. At that moment the green creature jumped out of the pond.

'Look! There it is!' Danny quacked.

'That isn't a fish. Fish don't jump,' said Derek.

'Fish don't have legs, either,' added Dinah.

So they went and told their mum all about it. But when Mrs Duck saw it, she burst out laughing.

'You sillies! That's a frog,' she said.

'Hi! I'm Frankie,' croaked the frog.

'Why, the last time I saw you, you were just a tadpole wriggling beneath a lily pad,' laughed Mrs Duck. 'Do come and tell me all your news.'

'Would you like a game of hide and seek, Frankie?' asked Danny after a while.

'I'd love to, if you'll teach me,' said Frankie.

Frankie learned quickly. He found good hiding places and his green skin made him hard to find. So they all played happily until it was time for tea.

C

edric had always been the biggest chick in the hen house, and he was becoming bigger every day. His legs were getting longer, his feathers smoother and he was growing a lovely red cockscomb on his head. He just could not wait to grow up!

'Soon I'll grow up and I'll make the loudest noise in the farmyard,' he would tell everyone. Then he would throw back his head . . . and make a rather odd sort of clucking sound! Then the other chicks laughed at him.

'You'll have to be patient,' his mother told him. 'Soon you'll be making a noise that will fill the farmyard from one end to the other.'

One morning, Cedric woke up earlier than usual, just as the dawn was breaking. He felt rather peculiar. He stretched his legs and strutted out into the yard. Then he climbed on top of the hen house, threw back his head and he crowed.

'Cock-a-doodle-do. Cock-a-doodle-do.' The sound just flowed from his throat and he crowed and crowed. All the animals crowded round, chattering excitedly. Cedric felt very proud. At last he had really grown up.

FISH OUT OF WATER

The farmer and his wife had a large pond full of goldfish at the end of their garden, next to the cows' field.

Tod the old toad lived nearby. Sometimes he sat under the rockery stones in the shade where it was cool and damp, and sometimes he swam in the pond.

Goldie, one of the young fish, was having a birthday party, and she wanted all the farm animals to come, but of course, she couldn't get out of the water to ask them.

Tod, who was swimming in the pond that morning, had a brilliant idea.

'I can go over to the farmyard and tell them all to join us,' he said.

That afternoon the farmer's wife looked out of her kitchen window and saw the sheepdog, the cat, the kittens, the piglets and the ducks stitting in a circle around the pond, and the cows and horses looking over the fence. What she didn't see was all the goldfish take a very deep breath and swim to the surface to sing 'Happy Birthday' to Goldie!

Garth Goose was the grooviest bird on the farm. In his glittering boots, shiny leather jacket and shades, he cut a dashing figure, strutting his way across the farmyard.

'You other birds are so uncool,' he would squawk. 'Soaring above the clouds is not for me – flying is so old hat. And as for you chickens – you're always flapping about. Why don't you just relax?'

Not for him the duck pond either – he might get his head wet and spoil his fashionable hairstyle. No, Garth Goose preferred to while away his time playing his guitar and composing new songs for famous pop stars. But today, Garth was having problems.

'I just can't get the tune right,' he said in frustration. Just then, a lark landed on a wall near Garth's head and began singing.

'That's beautiful!' Garth cried in astonishment.

By the evening, Garth and the lark had formed a great band with the chicken on drums and the ducks playing percussion.

'I was wrong about you other birds,' said Garth, ashamed. 'You sure are the coolest dudes a groovy goose like me could ever meet!'

It was Dilly Duckling's birthday.

'I hope it rains,' thought Dilly Duckling to herself. Dilly loved the rain. Her mum had promised her a birthday party, and all the ducklings on the farm had been invited. But the sun was shining, and Dilly Duckling felt sad.

'Nobody will come to my party,' she said.

'Cheer up,' said Mrs Duck. 'Perhaps it will rain after all. I'll ask the other animals.'

So Mrs Duck asked Jack Goat if it would rain that day, but he didn't know. She asked Delia Donkey, but she didn't know either.

Then Mrs Duck saw Mrs Cow lying down in the field. All the other cows were lying down, too.

'Why are you doing that?' asked Mrs Duck. 'Don't you feel well?'

'Cows always lie down when it is going to rain,' said Mrs Cow. 'Everybody knows that.'

'Thank you very much,' said Mrs Duck.

She told Dilly Duckling, who was delighted. That afternoon it rained and rained, and Dilly Duckling's friends came to the party and had a wonderful time.

'Clever Mrs Cow,' said Dilly Duckling.

Buttercup the cow sat under her favourite tree in acorn meadow with her mother, fluttering her exceptionally long eyelashes and painting her perfect little hooves. She was bored.

'There must be something more to life than eating grass and giving old farmer Hegarty his morning milk,' she sighed.

'Nonsense, my lovely,' mooed her mother. 'Eating grass and giving milk is what we cows do best.'

'Yes Mum, but *I* want to be special,' said Buttercup. 'Farmer Hegarty doesn't even notice me!'

The next day while the cows were being milked, a large black limousine drew up. The cow herd had never seen anything like it.

Suddenly, a rather fat man, with a big hat and a cigar the size of a milk churn, jumped out and pointed frantically at Buttercup.

'Oh those long eyelashes and pretty feet!' he exclaimed. 'You're perfect for my new film. Come with me Buttercup and I'll make you a star!'

And do you know what? He did! Next time you see a cow on television, look carefully at the long eyelashes, the elegant hooves and the gleaming hide. You never know, it might just be Buttercup.

When Tiny was born he lay on the straw in the farmyard and gazed round him. 'What am I?' he wondered.

He looked at the hens and ducks and geese and turkeys, but he hadn't any wings, so he wasn't a bird.

He saw a puppy and a kitten, but his legs were much longer than theirs and he didn't have claws.

Then he saw a piglet. It had a smooth twiddly tail and a flat nose, so he wasn't a pig.

Next came a cow. 'But my mummy hasn't got an udder,' he thought.

He saw an ewe with her lambs but their coats were curly, so he wasn't a sheep.

Two horses passed. 'That's better,' he thought, until one of them gave a loud whinny, which somehow didn't sound right.

Then his mummy twitched her long, long ears and gave a great bray of pride for her new baby. She pushed her nose under his soft furry tummy to help him to get up on to his long wobbly legs and said lovingly, 'Come on little donkey.'

Bonzo lay sleeping in his lovely new kennel. It would be hours before Carl the cockerel would be waking up the farmyard. Suddenly he awoke with a start! The hens were making a dreadful noise – squawking and flapping, scratching and rustling in the hen house.

He sniffed the night air. He could smell a fox!

He rushed round to the back of the hen house, barking loudly. There was the wild fox, digging under the wire fence, trying to get into the house. Bonzo ran up, barking and growling so fiercely that the fox ran off with his tail between his legs. He was so frightened he would never return to this farmyard again.

Farmer Tom ran up, wearing his pyjamas with his dressing gown flapping and his wellington boots on the wrong feet. He saw at once what had happened.

'Good boy, Bonzo,' he panted, patting Bonzo's head. 'Back to sleep now, old boy. He won't bother us again.'

When Bonzo woke again next morning, he sniffed the morning air. Outside his kennel there was a large juicy bone – a reward from Farmer Tom.

Edwin the little bull calf was feeling rather miserable.

'When you're bigger you will have to live in a field on your own and be fierce and chase people,' his cheeky twin sister told him.

'But I don't feel fierce,' Edwin said. 'I want to be friends with everyone. And I *don't* want to live in a field all by myself.'

But as time went on his mother had another calf, and the farmer had to find a new field for Edwin. However, he had a kind heart and knew how gentle Edwin was.

'We usually put a notice up on the field gate saying "Beware of the bull",' he said. 'But I don't think we need to do that with you, Edwin. How about sharing a field with old Peg the donkey? She'll keep you company and she's good at telling stories.'

Well, Edwin was so pleased the farmer didn't even have to lead him down to the field. He trotted right in front of him, mooing softly, down the lane to Peg's field!

One day the farmer noticed that Georgie Goat had eaten all the grass in the patch where he was tied up.

'That gives me an idea,' said the farmer. So he moved Georgie to the front garden of his house, and tied him to the fence.

'Now Georgie Goat will eat all the grass in my front garden, and I won't have to mow it. Georgie will save me lots of work.'

And that is exactly what happened. Georgie began to eat the grass. Later that day the farmer's wife hung her clean washing on the line.

'It's a warm, sunny day,' she said. 'My washing will soon be dry.'

But when she went back to collect her washing, it was all dirty again. Georgie Goat had butted it with his head, knocked it on the ground, and trampled all over it. He had even eaten two pairs of socks!

'Georgie Goat may have saved you a lot of work,' said the farmer's wife to her husband, 'but he has made an awful lot more for me!'

Eleanor the sheep was frantic. Where could her lamb have gone? She had only turned her back for a moment, she told Patrick the goat, and Lily had disappeared.

Patrick was a practical fellow.

'Don't worry, my dear,' he said. 'I have an idea,' and he ran to where Rover was sleeping in the sun.

'Quickly,' he said, shaking Rover to wake him. 'You must sniff out Lily Lamb's trail. She is lost.'

'But I'm a sheepdog,' complained Rover, 'not a blood-hound. I don't think I can find her.'

'Nonsense,' replied Patrick. 'You can do it.'

Rover was not so sure, but he was kind and always did his best. He began to sniff the ground, moving this way and that like a vacuum cleaner on a carpet.

Suddenly Rover took an extra large sniff and then began to weave his way across the field, through a hole in the fence and into the next field. They waited.

Then, from what seemed a long way away, there was a bark, and very soon another bark and a tiny bleat as Rover chased little Lily back to her mum.

'I told you you could do it, old man,' said Patrick. 'You can feel very proud of yourself.'

'So you did,' smiled Rover – who felt as proud of himself as the others did.

Dorothy sat sadly at the edge of the farmyard. She felt very alone without her mum.

'If only I could fly,' she sobbed to Pippin Pig, 'I could look down and I'd be able to see her.'

'I'll teach you to fly,' said Pippin hopefully. 'I'm sure you only have to flap your wings.' Dorothy tried, but her tiny, soft wings were just too small.

'Jump off the fence and flap your wings harder,' encouraged Pippin. The little bird hopped on to the fence and flapped. For a moment she hovered, then she crashed to the ground.

'One last try,' said Pippin. 'Climb up the oak tree and jump off – and flap your wings really hard.' Dorothy did just that – and rose high into the air! Pippin was delighted. Then suddenly, Dorothy dropped like a stone into the pond and disappeared!

'Oh no! Where are you?' Pippin wailed, peering into the water. But then he heard a voice cry,

'Look, Pippin. I've found my mum!' Pippin looked up. There was Dorothy paddling in the water with a family of ducks. She may not be big enough to fly just yet, but she could certainly swim!

Today we're going up to the hills to graze,' the mother sheep told her lambs one spring day. 'Make sure you follow each other's tail or you might get lost.'

Jed the sheepdog rounded them up and the farmer led the way. Lester, one of the lambs, had other ideas, however. Halfway up the steep track he thought he'd skip off and explore on his own.

'Come back here,' his mother and sister called, but he wouldn't listen. After a few minutes he looked round and couldn't see the others anywhere.

'Oh dear,' Lester wailed, 'I wish I'd listened to Mum.'

Just then, over the top of the hill, he saw Jed racing towards him. For once Lester was glad to see the bossy sheepdog.

'Come on,' Jed barked. 'Sheep always follow each other. You didn't, and that's how you got lost!'

Tracey was a very pretty sheep.

'Do look at my lovely curly coat,' she said to her brother Jason. 'I am so beautiful!' she baa-baa-baaed.

'You are very pretty,' said Jason, 'but I do wish you would stop telling everyone about it!'

'Look at me, do!' Tracey said to Pudgy Pig. 'Have you ever seen a finer sheep in all your life?'

'Yes, yes, very fine,' grunted Pudgy patiently.

Soon the spring came and the weather grew hotter.

'Time to shear the sheep,' said Farmer John. 'We will use their coats to make cardigans and jumpers.'

'Not me!' said Tracey. 'My coat is much too fine to be cut.' She pleaded so hard, with tears in her eyes, that eventually the farmer relented.

'Very well, Tracey,' he said. 'You may keep your coat, but I don't think you'll thank me for it!'

The summer came. The sun was hot and bright.

'I feel so hot and sticky,' moaned Tracey. 'I do wish I could take my coat off!'

'I thought you wanted to keep it,' smiled Jason.

'I did warn you,' chuckled the farmer.

'I am silly,' admitted Tracey. 'Next spring, I'll be happy to be sheared like all the others.'

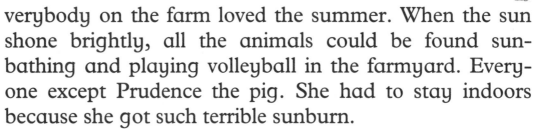

Everybody on the farm loved the summer. When the sun shone brightly, all the animals could be found sun-bathing and playing volleyball in the farmyard. Every-one except Prudence the pig. She had to stay indoors because she got such terrible sunburn.

'It's not fair,' she thought to herself. 'The other animals have wool or fur to protect them, and when the ducks get too hot they can go for a swim to cool down.'

The animals felt very sorry for Prudence. Suddenly, the swallows said they had an idea. They began flying back and forth collecting straw and weaving it together. The farmyard animals watched them and wondered how building a nest would help poor Prudence. But when the clever swallows had finished, their friends saw that it wasn't a nest they had been making but a beautiful big straw hat!

Now whenever Prudence goes out into the sun, she wears her hat to keep her in the shade and never gets sun-burned any more.

Cheeky was Molly Hen's naughtiest chick. One day he was playing hide and seek with his new friends, Paddles and Emmy the ducklings. It was great fun, rushing and quacking and clucking in and out of the long grasses. Soon they heard Clara calling her ducklings for lunch.

'See you, Cheeky,' they said, swimming happily off across the pond. Cheeky watched them.

'That looks fun,' he thought, and paddled off after them into the pond. The water was cold where it soaked his feathers but Cheeky went still deeper until suddenly he found himself sinking. He had never been so frightened! Then he felt something hard and firm nudge him back on to the bank. It was Clara, pushing him out with her beak.

'You silly chick,' she said, ruffling his wet feathers. 'Only ducklings can swim, my dear, not chicks.' Molly clucked over and snuggled him safely under her wing to dry in the warmth.

'I don't think I'll try swimming again,' said Cheeky, and they all laughed.

Charlie, you're late again!' said the teacher when Charlie the rabbit arrived half an hour late for school for the third time that week.

'I'm sorry, Sir,' said Charlie.

'What you need is an alarm clock,' said the teacher, and he was right.

So when school finished that day, Charlie went straightaway to see Mr Pig the shopkeeper. 'I want to buy the loudest alarm clock you have,' said Charlie.

The next morning, the alarm clock's loud bell woke Charlie up with a start.

'Hooray!' shouted Charlie. 'Today I won't be late!' He quickly got dressed and ran to school.

'I'm half an hour early today,' said Charlie to the teacher when he arrived.

'Well done, Charlie,' said his teacher. 'But it's Saturday – there's no school today.'

Poor old Charlie *was* embarrassed.

'But never mind,' said the teacher. 'At least you were early today.' And he gave Charlie a big vanilla ice cream as a reward.

I t's mine,' shrieked Flim.

'No, it's mine,' screamed Flam. All the other hens huddled at the other side of the hen house and covered their ears with their wings. Flim and Flam were making a dreadful din. Roger the rooster tried to ignore them, hoping they would get tired and stop arguing. But they only became noisier.

'What's up with you two?' he crowed.

'She's stolen my egg,' said Flim.

'No, she's stolen *my* egg,' said Flam. Roger watched as each hen tried to sit on the same egg by pushing the other one off.

'Stop doing that or you'll break the egg,' he cried. Flim jumped up quick as a flash and said, 'Oh. I hadn't thought of that.' But Flam sat down on the egg and said, 'I don't care. It's mine. I can do what I like with it.'

Roger cleared his throat, 'Cock-a-doodle-do,' and said, 'Flam, get off that egg. Flim cares about it more than you, so from now on it belongs to her.'

The hens cheered, 'Wise Roger!' and settled down on to their nests for a peaceful sleep.

Sometimes Edward Seagull would stop by the sty. If he was in a good mood, he would tell tales of the sea. Pepper loved to listen. She would gaze at the gull, eyes glowing, listening to his stories of exotic places.

One night, after a visit from Edward, she thought she heard a voice in her ear. 'Swim, swim,' it said.

'I can't!' said Pepper. 'Anyway, I'm not in water.'

'Try,' said the little voice.

Pepper kicked her trotters, and found to her surprise that she *was* swimming – and the water *was* salty! She turned to see a little piglet about her size – with a fish's tail! She could hardly believe it.

'I'm a mer-pig,' said the creature. 'I'm going to show you around under the sea. You'll be safe with me.'

Together they explored beneath the waves, swimming with the fish and sending surprised crabs scuttling across the sea bed.

'I must take you home now,' said the Mer-pig. 'But keep this shell to remind you of your magic adventure.'

Next morning Pepper woke up in her straw bed. She could not wait to tell her family about her adventure.

'Don't be silly!' they scoffed. 'There's no such thing as a mer-pig!' Pepper held her shell tightly. She knew that the magic adventure had really happened.

Graham the turkey was given a bright red sledge for Christmas. It was the first time he had ever seen one.

'Brilliant!' he gobbled excitedly. 'But what is it for?' he asked his mum.

'Well dear,' Mrs Turkey explained. 'You carry the sledge to the top of the hill and sit on it. Then you slide all the way to the bottom.'

'Wow!' said Graham. 'Thank you, Mum,' and off he went to try it.

An hour later, Graham returned, puffed out and rather angry.

'It doesn't work!' he said.

'Oh you silly turkey,' his mum laughed. 'You need to wait for the snow first!'

The next morning, snow fell all around the farm and Mrs Turkey took Graham and his sledge right to the top of the hill again. This time when Graham sat on his sledge the slippery snow made the sledge slide.

'Wheeee!' he yelled, all the long way to the bottom.

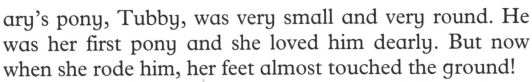

Mary's pony, Tubby, was very small and very round. He was her first pony and she loved him dearly. But now when she rode him, her feet almost touched the ground!

'We must do something about that pony,' Dad said.

A few weeks later, it was Mary's birthday. She woke up very excited and looked around the room. But there was not a present in sight! Slowly and sadly, she got dressed. Reaching for her boots she noticed a scrap of paper fixed to some yarn. 'Follow me,' it said.

So she followed the yarn down the stairs, into the yard and to the stables. There she found a lovely new pony.

'Surprise!' said Mum and Dad. 'His name is Thunderbolt. Happy birthday!'

'Dad, he's fantastic,' gasped Mary. 'Look at his long legs and his silvery mane!'

They saddled up Thunderbolt and Mary mounted his back. At once, he set off across the yard and into the field from where Tubby watched the activity. Mary did not even look at him. His head drooped.

'I only have stumpy legs and a stubbly mane,' he said sadly. But Thunderbolt was going too fast.

'Help!' cried Mary. Thunderbolt stopped dead at a hedge and Mary was thrown with a bump. She started to cry. Tubby trotted up and licked away the tears.

'Oh, Tubby, you are so kind and gentle,' she said. 'And I did not even pat you today of all days. However big I grow, you will always be my favourite.'

W hat's on the other side of the fence?' asked Lewis.

'You'll find out when you've grown up a bit,' his mother replied. 'Don't be such a nosy lamb!'

But that answer didn't satisfy Lewis. He wanted to know NOW!

He asked the goats and the ducks. He even asked the snooty geese, but no one would tell him.

'Okay!' he thought angrily. 'I'll just have to find out for myself,' and off he walked. In the corner of the field someone had left an old mattress.

'Great!' thought Lewis. 'A trampoline!'

He jumped on to the mattress and began to bounce higher and higher. 'Now – I – can – see – over – the – fence!' he panted.

Suddenly he felt hot breath on his face. Lewis was eye to eye with the biggest, ugliest and fiercest bull on the farm! He fell back on to the mattress with a thump.

'I think I'll stay on this side of the fence until I'm a bit bigger,' he told his mother.

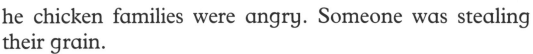

The chicken families were angry. Someone was stealing their grain.

'We must organise a patrol,' said the Colonel, who was the oldest cockerel on the farm, 'and keep a night watch to catch the thief!'

Later that night, the Colonel and his eldest son were patrolling up and down the farmyard when they heard a scratching noise coming from behind the bags of grain.

'Quick!' hissed the Colonel. 'The thief's over there!'

They ran over to the bags, pulled them out of the way and the Colonel shone his torch into the corner. Sitting, blinking in the bright light, was Heather Hen, munching her way through a large bowl of grain.

'But I'm so hungry!' Heather cried 'My older brothers always get to the food before I do and there's never any left for me.'

The Colonel took Heather back to her parents, and they promised her that she could have her very own bowl of grain from then on.

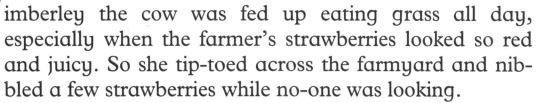

Kimberley the cow was fed up eating grass all day, especially when the farmer's strawberries looked so red and juicy. So she tip-toed across the farmyard and nibbled a few strawberries while no-one was looking.

The next day the farmer was hopping mad.

'Look at my strawberry patch,' he cried. 'You've trampled on it and turned my strawberries into mush.'

The farmer picked up all the crushed strawberries and put them into a bucket to make strawberry jam. Then he went into the farmhouse to wash his hands. Just then his wife came out and started to milk Kimberley. But she forgot to look inside the bucket and squirted Kimberley's milk right on top of the mushy strawberries!

When she had finished milking Kimberley, the farmer's wife looked into the bucket and screamed! The farmer ran out to see what all the fuss was about.

'Look,' said the farmer's wife, 'Kimberley has eaten so many strawberries she's made strawberry milk shake!' The farmer laughed and laughed! And when he explained what had happened his wife laughed too. And as for the milk shake – it was delicious!

Everyone in the pig pen was fast asleep – except Pickle. As soon as the sun came up he squealed, 'It's my birthday. Wake up everyone. Wake up!' But everyone stayed fast asleep, so Pickle squeezed under the pig pen gate and escaped into the farmyard to find a friend.

First he met Henry the horse, but Henry trotted past in a great hurry. Next he met Mandy the hen, but she rushed out of sight without even saying hello. Then he met Chloe the lamb, but Chloe skipped past without stopping.

Pickle turned back home, his tail drooping between his legs. 'No-one cares about my birthday,' he said to himself. But when Pickle arrived back home to the pig pen it was empty! 'Hello, anyone there!' he called. No-one answered.

Suddenly Henry, Mandy, Chloe and all the pigs jumped out from nowhere and shouted, 'Surprise, surprise. Happy Birthday, Pickle.' Pickle felt happy again!

Barney, the farm dog, was sleeping peacefully by his kennel in the corner of the farmyard. His snoring was so loud he didn't hear the tiny ducklings, Mark and Lizzie, creep over to where he lay in the shade. They had decided that Barney's huge water bowl was just what they needed on this hot summer's day – their own private swimming pool!

They slipped over the rim of the bowl and into the lovely, cool water. Bobbing and diving, splishing and splashing, they were so excited chasing each other around they didn't notice that Barney was beginning to stir and stretch.

'Aaaahh!' Barney yawned. 'Time for a drink. My mouth is so dry!'

With a big slurp, Barney dipped his tongue into the water bowl. 'Erggh!' he spluttered. 'I almost swallowed those furry lumps.' Mark and Lizzie got a terrible fright!

Barney carried the two ducklings back to the farm pond sitting on his head.

'That's the last time you go swimming in my water bowl,' he said.

The kittens' bedroom was in a dreadful mess again. Their clothes were in a pile by the door, they'd spread paintings on the floor to dry, and there were so many toys and books on the carpet that it was hard to find any clear space to walk on.

Poor Mrs Clara Cat didn't know what to do. How could she persuade her kittens to keep their room tidy?

Today they were going to Tanya Turkey's birthday party. They were going to wear their new blue dresses, which had pink ribbon threaded round the sleeves. The kittens loved them – but they couldn't find them anywhere. They looked and looked but their room was so untidy it was almost impossible to find anything.

Just then they caught sight of the pink ribbon underneath a pile of books. They pulled – and the jam jar of dirty water they had been painting with tipped all over their new dresses.

'Now you know why it's important to keep your room tidy,' their mother said. 'You'll just have to go to the party in your old dresses.' From then on the kittens kept their room tidy – well, most of the time anyway.

It was Farm Fun Day and the wheelbarrow race was about to begin. Six wheelbarrows were lined up at the starting tape and the first team to push their barrow to the fence would win a huge jar of sweets.

The duck team were sure they would win as they had been practising for weeks. But they didn't know that the pig's team had a secret weapon – tractor grease – which they had spread along the race track.

The race began and all the animals began shouting for their favourite teams. The ducks' barrow was soon in the lead, when – DISASTER! Their barrow hit the patch of grease and went skidding into the pond. The grease patch had spread across the farmyard and the pigs also ran straight into it. Squealing loudly, they too went headlong into the pond.

The goats who were judging the race declared that no one had won and no one had lost. So the jar of sweets was shared between the teams after the pigs had apologised for trying to cheat and cleared up the huge mess they caused.

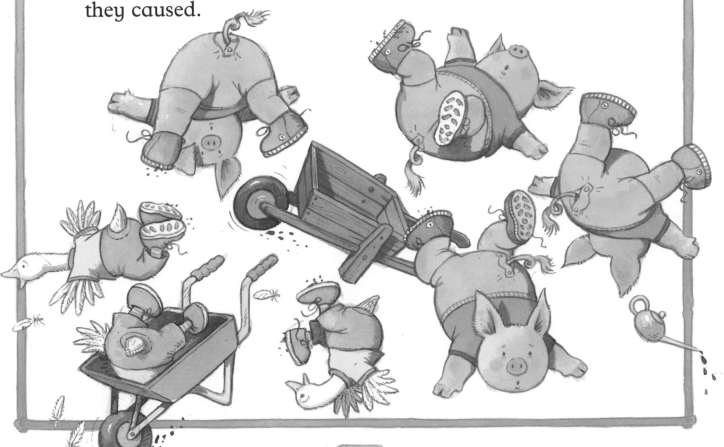

One day a strange-looking animal appeared in the farm-yard. Everyone clustered around the newcomer and stared. Gary the goat, who wasn't scared of anything, moved to the front of the crowd. He cleared his throat and said loudly, 'So who are you?'

'I'm Jane. I'm a guinea pig,' said the stranger.

'She doesn't look much like a pig to me,' muttered one of the geese.

'I live in the house down the road, but I'm fed up with our tiny garden,' said Jane. 'Could I stay here?'

'Can she live with us, Mummy?' one of the piglets squealed, jumping up and down.

'I think your mummy will be worried about you,' the mother pig said kindly. 'Stay for some tea and then – we'll see.'

Jane happily settled down to share the piglets' tea. Meanwhile, Mrs Pig sent Gary to bring Jane's mum down to the farmyard.

It was starting to get dark as they arrived. Jane was beginning to wonder whether she wanted to stay in the farmyard after all. She felt rather small.

'I think visiting is best,' she said, as she snuggled up closely to her mum on Gary's back for the journey home.

The young farm animals were putting up their tents in Bluebell Wood. They were on a camping weekend with their schoolteacher, Mr Gander.

They gathered around the camping stove and tucked in to big plates of potatoes and beans. After they had eaten, everyone took it in turns to tell a story. Some of the tales were very scary – all about ghosts in the woods.

Later that night, Mr Gander thought he heard some noises. He poked his beak through his tent flap and saw a very strange shape sticking out of the hens' tent.

'Who's that, who's that?' he shouted and ran over, flapping his wings.

Brian, one of the cows, was trying to get into the hens' tent, but he was stuck in the zipped flap which wouldn't open wide enough to let him in.

'I was scared of the ghosts,' he explained to Mr Gander after he had been rescued, 'And I thought it was your tent.'

'Well, you're safe now,' smiled his teacher. 'I'll keep watch for any ghosts!'

Owen the pig looked over the wall of his sty.

'Yum! Yum! Yum!' he said. The tree by his sty was covered in big rosy apples. Some of the apples had fallen on to the grass.

'If only!' sighed Owen. 'If only I could get out of my sty and eat some of those juicy apples!'

'Dinner time, Owen!' shouted Sally the farmer's daughter. 'I have brought your pig feed and scraps from the kitchen. There's potato chips, porridge and cornflakes! All your favourites!' Owen poked his long pink snout in his trough.

'Huh!' he snorted. 'I am fed up with scraps!' . . . but he gobbled and slurped and snorted and ate them all up just the same.

Then Owen noticed Sally had left the latch off his gate. He pushed the gate gently with his trotter. The gate fell open!

'Yippee!' said Owen as he scurried over to the bottom of the apple tree.

'Yum! Yum! Yum!' he snorted with delight as he gobbled up the juicy red apples.

But . . . oh dear! . . . What a terrible tummy ache he had that night!

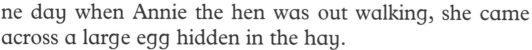

One day when Annie the hen was out walking, she came across a large egg hidden in the hay.

'I wonder who this belongs to,' she thought. Since no-one seemed to want it, she decided to sit on it. The other hens told her she shouldn't sit on strange eggs, but Annie ignored them. She sat on the egg for a very long time and looked after it carefully.

One exciting day, she felt the egg moving beneath her. She jumped up, and as she watched, the egg cracked and, slowly but surely, out came a tiny and very hungry chick.

Annie fed her chick big, juicy worms, as many as she could find. But still the chick was hungry. She had a huge beak and swallowed the worms whole. She grew bigger and bigger. When she was almost as big as Annie she started flapping her wings. Annie couldn't teach her to fly because she did not know how.

'Oh dear,' sighed Annie, 'what am I to do?'

Then she had an idea. Perhaps her friends at the pond would help. So Annie led the chick down there. When the ducks saw the chick they quacked and quacked! Annie saw her mistake at once. The chick was, in fact, a baby duck! She gave Annie a big hug.

'I'll come back and visit you soon,' she called, as she swam off happily with the other ducks.

Dan and Dennis, the black and white calves, had been pestering their mother all day asking if they could sleep in their little tent that night.

'Oh please,' they begged – again, 'it's a lovely warm evening, perfect for camping.'

'Very well', their mother said, 'let's see how you get on tonight.'

So after tea Dan and Dennis put the tent up in the field next to their barn. Then they snuggled into their sleeping bags and settled down for the night.

At home they were usually asleep as soon as their heads touched the pillow, but tonight they just couldn't sleep. It was very dark, and they heard funny noises which sounded like ghosts howling, not like the soft moo-ing of the other cows at night.

Just then their mother popped her head through the tent flap.

'Are you all right?' she said.

'Yes,' said Dan and Dennis together, 'but perhaps we'll come back into the barn. We'll camp out another night.'

Herbert, the old sheepdog, lay in the sun, snoring.

'Get up, Herbert!' shouted the farmer. 'The sheep have to be rounded up and put in their pen.'

'Go away,' barked Herbert.

'Come on, lad,' encouraged the farmer, tugging at Herbert's collar.

'Please go away,' growled Herbert. 'I am comfortable lying in the sun and I do not care any more about those silly sheep.'

'What a lazy dog you are,' said the farmer crossly. Then he thought for a moment. 'Well,' he said. 'I suppose you must be getting on in years. But while you are my sheepdog, you have to earn your keep.'

Reluctantly, Herbert rounded up the sheep. When his work was done he found a nice warm spot in the barn and fell fast asleep.

When he woke up, the sun was already high in the sky and the farmer was nowhere to be found. He did not even come to let the sheep out of the pen. Then early in the afternoon he drove back into the yard, opened the back door of the truck – and what should bound out but a handsome young sheepdog.

'Meet the new sheepdog,' said the farmer, tickling Herbert in his favourite spot behind the ears. 'I think you've earned your retirement. You can sleep in the sun for as long as you like.'

Gloria lamb's auntie and uncle and her cousin Luke were coming for tea. Gloria's mum had made a delicious chocolate cake.

'When are they coming, Mum?' Gloria asked for the umpteenth time. She couldn't wait to start eating!

At last the doorbell rang. But the grown-ups didn't want tea straightaway. They sent Gloria and Luke out to play. Gloria could see the lovely cake through the kitchen window.

'I'm just getting a drink of water,' she told Luke as she went into the kitchen.

The chocolate cake looked beautiful.

'Nobody will notice if I eat a tiny piece,' Gloria thought. Luke was busy kicking a football about the yard. Gloria broke off the cake and popped it into her mouth. It tasted wonderful. Another bit had come loose, so she ate that too. Then she went back outside.

'Was it good?' asked Luke.

'How did you guess?' Gloria asked in surprise.

'Easy!' said Luke. 'You forgot to lick the crumbs off your lips. But I'd have known anyway.' He winked. 'I always test the cake first when we have visitors!'

Everyone on the farm liked Hannah. But her sisters laughed at her because she was skinny.

'You are all white feathers and bone,' said Edna.

'It's a pity you're not fat and brown like us,' said Harriet as she squeezed into her nest.

One day all three hens were filled with excitement, for they had all laid their very own egg!

'Oooh, we're going to have baby chicks,' said Edna.

'I can't wait,' said Harriet.

Hannah smiled to herself and felt her egg beneath her, warm and smooth.

A couple of weeks later, Edna's egg began to crack from the inside – crick, crock, crack. A tiny ball of yellow feathers appeared. Then Harriet's egg started to do the same – crick, crock, crack. A fuzzy yellow ball stepped out. Everyone looked at Hannah and her egg. Nothing happened. They waited. Still nothing happened.

'Perhaps you are too skinny to keep it warm like we can,' sniffed Harriet.

Hannah took no notice. She just sat there until a few days later she heard – crick, crock, crack. And out from the egg popped not one but two little chicks. Hannah the skinny hen had twins!

It was almost Christmas, the snow was deep, and the young animals on the farm were very excited.

Their parents were very busy cooking mince pies and wrapping presents so they suggested the youngsters go out sledging.

Katie and Kathryn, the piglets, brought their big sledge, and everyone had a wonderful time zooming down the high bank near the wood.

When they'd all had lots of turns, the youngsters set off for home. Just then Ellen the lamb gave a shout.

'Wait a minute,' she said, staring at a holly tree with lots of lovely red berries. 'Let's put some of this holly on to the sledge and take it home to decorate the barn for our Christmas celebrations.'

And so they did. When all the animals sat down at the long table in the barn for their Christmas dinner, the grown-ups agreed that they had never seen the barn looking so pretty!

Benjamin Piglet was very proud of his curly tail.

'Your tail is completely straight,' he said to his friend James Donkey. 'It's not pretty and curly like mine.'

'My tail is more useful than yours,' said James.

Benjamin Piglet laughed. 'Don't be silly,' he said. 'You are just envious.'

Just then Wally Wasp flew past. He was feeling tired, so he stopped to have a rest on Benjamin's back. Benjamin tried to shake him off. Wally Wasp got angry, and stung him.

'Ow, ow,' shrieked Benjamin. 'That hurt!'

Wally Wasp decided to rest somewhere else. This time he landed on the back of James Donkey.

'Let me have a good, comfy sleep,' said Wally, 'or I'll sting you.' But James swished his long, straight tail and knocked Wally off his back. Wally Wasp was so frightened he flew away.

'I told you my straight tail was more useful than your curly one,' said James to Benjamin. 'And I was right!'

The first thing Splodge did when she was allowed out to explore the farmyard was climb a tree. She loved scrambling up the rough bark. It was wonderful to scratch her neck on the stiff twigs. And the feel of the dappled sunlight warming her fur as she stretched out on a branch was bliss.

One wet day, the kittens were talking about the places they had discovered around the farm.

'My favourite place is the barn,' said Blackie. 'You can play with the corn and sleep in the straw.'

'I like the yard best,' said Snowy. 'It's fun playing with the chicks.'

'The trees are definitely the best place for me,' Splodge said. 'But I do wish there were more of them.'

Just then their mother arrived and heard them.

'Now you are bigger you can go a little further tomorrow,' she smiled. 'Blackie can go to the big hay barn in the field. Snowy can try the cowsheds to play with the calves. And Splodge, you can squeeze under the fence by the pond and see what you find.'

Next morning, the kittens couldn't wait to explore. Splodge crouched very low and scrambled under the fence, as her mother had told her, to find what from then on was her most favourite place – the orchard!

Uncle Billy said he would bring special fireworks to our birthday picnic,' Natalie said to Michael. 'But if we get a shower of rain, there'll be no picnic.'

'Here he comes,' said Michael, as Uncle Billy Goat trotted towards them with a bag over his shoulder.

'Have you got lots of noisy bangers?' asked Michael. 'And some pretty coloured ones?' said Natalie.

'No,' said Billy with the hint of a smile. 'Just a few little rockets.' The twins tried not to look sad.

'Do you think it will rain?' they asked.

'Oh yes,' he replied cheerfully. 'It will rain!' The twins looked at each other and frowned.

They started collecting sticks to build a bonfire, then set out the picnic. Billy brought out his rockets, picked some flowers and blew up some balloons. He would not let them watch what he did with them!

WHOOSH! A rocket shot into the air, lifting with it a bunch of colourful flowers. As the rocket burst into stars, red, yellow and blue flowers showered down.

WHIZZ! A green balloon was lifted up on the next rocket. The sparks burst the balloon with a huge BANG!

'Lovely,' cried Natalie.

'Brilliant,' shouted Michael. The twins agreed they were the best fireworks anyone could wish for.

Mrs Amy Duck had been taking her family of ducklings to the farm pond every day for the past week to practise their swimming.

They were all coming along very well – all except Monty. He refused to get into the water. 'I know I'll hate it,' he said. 'Why must I learn to swim? I'd much rather stay dry.'

'All ducks swim,' said his mother, who by this time was getting more than a little impatient.

Still Monty refused to put a foot in. Now it happened to be a very windy day, and as he waddled along the side watching his brothers and sisters swimming, a strong gust of wind suddenly got under his feathers, lifted him up and dropped him into the pond!

The water felt soft and silky all around him, and Monty found that his webbed feet were already pushing him quickly towards the others.

'Perhaps I will learn to swim after all!' he giggled.

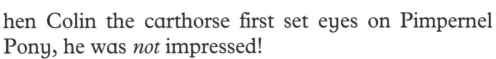

When Colin the carthorse first set eyes on Pimpernel Pony, he was *not* impressed!

'What a funny little thing you are,' he said. 'Why, your head hardly comes up to my shoulder!'

'Well, you're the size of a mammoth!' retorted Pimpernel. 'You and your great shaggy feet!'

So Colin went to one end of the field, and Pimpernel to the other. And that is where they stayed all through the spring! Then came the hot weather, and with the hot weather came – flies! The flies buzzed all round Colin at his end of the field, and all round Pimpernel at hers.

Both of them flicked at the flies with their tails, but those flies just kept on coming . . .

'One tail isn't enough for all these flies,' grumbled Colin, looking down the field at Pimpernel.

'I need some help with these terrible flies,' wailed Pimpernel, looking up the field at Colin.

And by the end of the afternoon they were standing together, head to tail, flicking their tails in turn. And they had a lot of talking to catch up on, too!

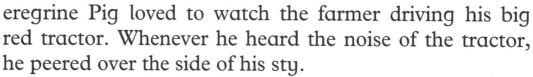

Peregrine Pig loved to watch the farmer driving his big red tractor. Whenever he heard the noise of the tractor, he peered over the side of his sty.

'I'd love to drive that tractor,' he told his friends. 'And I'm sure I could. It looks very easy.'

'Don't be silly!' they scoffed. 'You're a pig. You can't drive tractors!'

One day the farmer drove into the yard – then dashed into the farmhouse, leaving the tractor engine running.

Peregrine watched it roaring in the yard – suddenly he could bear it no longer. Leaping out of his sty, he ran and jumped up into the cab. As he did so, he knocked a blue lever on the tractor and it began – to move! He was driving!

But Peregrine's joy quickly turned to horror. The tractor was going straight for the pig sties. And before he could squeak 'Help!' it drove smack into the side of his little home. CRASH!

The farmer was furious! 'You're a very naughty pig!' he said. 'And I can't repair your sty for at least a week.' So for a time Peregrine had nowhere to live. And he decided – very wisely – to leave the driving to the farmer in future.

I t was such a good bone,' muttered Patch the farm dog as the mud sprayed up behind his digging feet. 'I know I buried it somewhere here. I'll try one more hole . . .' Patch continued to dig. 'I wish these flowers were not in the way,' he grumbled. But then there was a shout!

'You bad dog!' It was Mrs Plum, the farmer's wife. 'Look at the flowers! I'll have to replant them all.'

Patch hid by the barn. He could hear her talking crossly to herself, and when he felt brave enough to peer out from his hiding place he saw that she had replanted the flowers and was going back to the house.

He waited. He waited a bit longer. But he could not resist one last attempt to find his bone. Mud and flowers flew as he dug a really deep hole in the middle of the flower bed. There was something there! Something hard! Was it his bone? No, it was small, hard yellow things, and they tasted – ugh horrible!

'You wicked dog!' Patch was startled and started to run away. 'This time I'm going to tie you up and you'll wait a long time until I give you another . . .'

As Mrs Plum reached the hole, she stopped, bent down, and picked up the shiny things.

'Well, I never,' she said. 'Old Mr Plum was right after all. I'd never have believed it, Patch, but you have found treasure! You clever boy!' And, of course, his reward was – a great, big, juicy bone.

Laurie the lamb thought she was so beautiful that she spent hours gazing at her reflection in the pond. When the other lambs asked her to join in their games, Laurie would turn up her pretty nose and say,

'No thank you. I don't want to get muddy!'

One day, Laurie was staring at the water when she caught sight of a little white lamb every bit as beautiful as herself, trotting past.

'Hello,' said Laurie, spinning round quickly to catch sight of the lamb. But as she turned, she slipped and fell headlong into the water with a splosh!

Her friends rushed over to see what the noise was about as Laurie pulled herself, dripping, from the pond.

'Oh dear, look at Laurie,' said one lamb, finding it hard not to laugh. The others tried not to giggle. Laurie looked at herself in the water – what a sight!

'Aaah,' she gasped, but soon even she could not help laughing. 'I look like a haystack!' she giggled. At that all the other lambs burst out laughing – and Laurie never wasted her time staring into the water again. It was too much fun playing games.

All the animals on the farm were enjoying a day trip to the seaside.

Mr Samuel Horse drove their bus, and by eleven o'clock everyone was enjoying themselves on the beach. The grown-ups sat in their deck-chairs, the puppies chased off into the sea, and the young sheep and kittens built a sandcastle. Thomas the donkey gave everyone rides, the calves explored rockpools, and the piglets collected shells.

Mrs Rebecca Horse had brought two picnic baskets full of delicious things to eat, and after lunch Jessica Pig fetched ice cream for everyone.

But the piglets had collected so many shells they couldn't carry them in their buckets.

'What can we do?' they wailed. 'We don't want to leave them behind.'

Thomas came to the rescue. 'I can carry all sorts of things. Put the shells into the empty picnic baskets and tie them on to my back. I'll carry them up the cliff path to our bus.' And he did just that!

Pattie Pig shared a sty with a much bigger pig called Hattie. They got on very well – apart from one thing. Hattie was very, very greedy!

When dinner-time came, she would rush over and grab all the nicest things – and Pattie was left with just the potato peelings.

'It's not fair you grabbing the best things all the time,' Pattie grumbled.

'I'm a bigger pig,' boomed Hattie. 'And I need more food. It's **quite** fair!'

One day the pigs' dinner came – topped with glistening red jam!

'Jam!' roared Hattie and, pushing Pattie aside as usual, she started gobbling it up.

But in her greed Hattie didn't notice something. Sitting on the strawberry jam was a large stripy wasp – which promptly stung her on the snout!

'Ow, ow, ow!' screamed Hattie.

'Serves you right for being so greedy,' said the other farm animals.

After that Hattie always let Pattie have **some** of the nicer things!

an we play with Rosie?' Dickon asked his father.

'I don't think so,' he said. 'You know she's a greedy nuisance. We named her because she ate my roses.'

'Please, Dad,' begged Dickon and his sister Linda.

'Oh, all right then,' said the farmer. 'But don't let that goat near my roses.'

The children took Rosie into the garden. Linda stroked her soft white fur while Dickon played with her grizzly white beard.

'She's a sweet goat. Dad is wrong to think she's greedy,' said Dickon. 'I don't think she's a nuisance!'

Soon the children tired of playing with her. They lay on the lawn and made daisy chains. Rosie wandered off. She saw the farmer's rose bushes.

'Delicious,' she bleated and hurried over to them. Crunch . . . munch . . . Rosie gobbled up the red roses. Then she ate the yellow roses. Then she ate the pink roses! Suddenly Dickon noticed Rosie was missing.

'She was here a minute ago!' said Linda.

When Dad returned from the milking, he saw Rosie in the garden – with the very last pink rose in her mouth!

'Dickon! Linda!' he shouted, but they were nowhere to be found. They hid in the shed until he calmed down. But he never let them play with Rosie again.

The white doves hadn't lived on the farm for long. The farmer had built them a wooden house – called the dove-cote – high on the roof of the barn.

Once a week a van came to the farm delivering special cattle food to the farmer, and the doves saw a way of making friends with the other animals. As soon as they saw the van in the distance, they flew down to the cows and said, 'The man with your food is on his way. Hurry across the field to the trough where the farmer puts it.'

The cows set off, one following the other, so that by the time the farmer reached the trough, they were waiting for him – week after week, after week.

'Do you know,' the farmer said to his wife, 'our cows are so clever, they even seem to know which day of the week their special food arrives.'

And from that day on, the doves became part of the happy farmyard family!

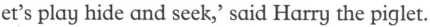

Let's play hide and seek,' said Harry the piglet.

'Okay,' agreed his sister Debbie. 'Who will hide?'

'I will,' announced Harry. 'Shut your eyes and count to ten – and no peeping!'

'You are the one who peeps,' answered Debbie crossly. 'I never peep.' *One, two three . . .*

Harry wondered where to go. He looked round the farmyard. Behind the milk churn? No, she would look there first. *Four, five, six . . .* Under the hen coop? No, the hens would squawk. *Seven, eight, nine . . .*

'I know,' he decided. 'I'll hide in the barn. It will be nice and warm in there.' He dashed into the barn just as Debbie shouted, '*Ten!* Ready or not, here I come.'

Suddenly a gust of wind blew the door shut with a BANG! Harry was trapped. It was dark. Something rustled in the straw. He felt frightened. Debbie would never find him here.

'Harry!' It was Debbie's voice. Where was she? 'There's a loose plank here,' she said. Harry could see a chink of light. Puffing and pushing with all his might he was soon free.

'Thank you,' smiled Harry. Debbie looked downcast.

'I peeped,' she admitted.

'Never mind,' said Harry. 'I'm very glad you did!'

Nell, the old carthorse, was telling her great granddaughter, Juniper, all about the days when she had pulled the plough and the hay cart on the farm. The foal had only ever seen the tractor do this.

'Oh, please tell me about the lovely harness you wore, and the horse brasses and the ribbons,' she begged. So Nell told her all over again.

'I wish I could have seen how you looked,' Juniper sighed. 'Just be patient,' said Nell, smiling a secret smile.

Every summer, the farmer and his family organised a village show in the field near the stream. Juniper watched in amazement as Nell was brushed till her coat shone. Jingling harness and horse brasses with bells were put on her, and her mane and tail were plaited with red and blue ribbons. She even had little red caps over her ears to keep the flies away.

And no one was prouder than Juniper as she watched Nell pull a lovely old haycart into the show ring!

The animals were so excited. Their favourite day of the year had almost arrived. The posters had been put up weeks before. The sheds had been tidied and the gates mended. The only trouble was that the young animals had no idea what was going on.

'Please tell us,' they begged, but the reply was always the same, 'Be patient! It's worth waiting for.'

Peter Puppy tried to hide in the straw and listen to the horses, but he sneezed and they shooed him away.

Albert Chick felt sure he would hear something when he hid under the leaves by the ducks' pond, but they only talked about whose feathers were the loveliest.

Melissa Mouse thought she had a better chance than anyone to creep up on the grown-ups and hear some news, but Tom Cat kept a beady, watchful eye on her all the time.

When the day finally came, the excitement was almost too much to bear.

'Ready, team?' said Farmer Chris as he pegged back the big farm gates. There was a chorus of happy noises from all the animals as a steady stream of children and their families came in to look round the farm and to stroke and pet and feed the animals. And the young ones agreed that it was definitely worth waiting for!

etty Bat was flying around the farm at night. She had been asleep all day, but now she thought she would like to visit her friends. It was a very windy night, and all the trees were swaying and shaking their branches.

Betty flew to the top of the tree where Cindy Sparrow lived. But her nest was no longer there. It had been blown out of the tree by the wind.

'Oh, what am I to do?' cried Cindy Sparrow. 'I have nowhere to live.'

'Don't worry,' said Betty Bat. 'You can come home with me for tonight.' Cindy Sparrow was still frightened.

'Won't the wind blow your nest down too?' she asked. Betty Bat just laughed.

She took her friend back to the barn where she lived. They flew high up to the beams beneath the roof.

'We'll be safe here,' said Betty Bat.

So Betty Bat hung upside down on the beam, and Cindy Sparrow sat beside her.

The wind whistled and roared, but it didn't worry them one bit!

One evening Penelope Pig was lying on her back looking at the moon.

'I wonder what it could be,' she thought. So she asked Milly the cow.

'Milly, I've been wondering – what is the moon?'

'Oh, that's simple,' Milly replied. 'The moon is a huge bucket of milk.'

To Penelope this seemed a little strange so she asked Shirley the sheep.

'Shirley, can you tell me what the moon is?'

'Easy,' said Shirley. 'It's a giant white fleece.'

Now Penelope was really confused so she asked Sophie the hen.

'Sophie, do you know what the moon is?'

'It's obvious, isn't it?' Sophie replied. 'It's a humungous white egg.'

By now Penelope did not know what to think, so she told her mother what everyone had said.

'But who is telling the truth?' she asked.

'They are all telling the truth,' smiled her mother. 'Since none of us really know what the moon is, it can be whatever we want it to be.'

What would you like the moon to be?

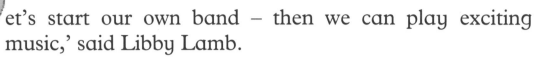

Let's start our own band – then we can play exciting music,' said Libby Lamb.

'Don't be silly,' said her friend Simon Calf. 'How can we play music without instruments?'

'We can make our own,' she said. Libby jumped on top of an old oil drum and danced around, making a loud drumming noise. Then she jumped on to a smaller drum next to it that made a different, deeper, sound. 'There,' she said. 'I'm the drummer.'

'You can blow these,' said Libby, pointing excitedly to some plastic water pipes that had been left in the farm-yard. Simon huffed and puffed and at last managed to make some sounds.

'What's all that noise?' asked Henry Hedgehog, rustling through the dry leaves under the hedge.

'Hey, that sounds great!' laughed Libby. 'Come and join our band.'

'This looks fun,' said Gerald Goat. 'Can I play the guitar?' And he started to pluck the wire fence where it ran past the wooden barn.

What a wonderful time they all had drumming, blowing, rustling and plucking!

'I think we are so good,' announced Libby, 'that *we* ought to make a record!'

Jemima, the old tabby farm cat, was sitting on the farm-yard wall with her kittens.

'Tonight's bath night, so I'm going to teach you how to wash yourselves,' she said. 'Cats like to be clean but it takes a bit of practice. Come down off the wall and I'll show you how to do it.'

Three of the kittens jumped down after their mother, but the fourth, Terry, had other ideas. He'd seen two birds splashing about in a puddle having a bath. 'That looks much more fun, I think I'll try that.'

He leapt off the wall, ran towards the puddle and jumped in with a splash. 'Oh, it's horrible,' he squealed. 'My fur is all wet and my tail's soggy!'

From the entrance to the barn his mother and brothers laughed. 'I should leave water to the birds,' Jemima said. 'Cats don't like to get wet. Now shake the water off your paws, come here and I'll start the lesson again!'

Leyla and Esther, the rabbit twins, were a little nervous about starting school. They had often seen the school teacher, Mrs Turkey, in the farmyard. She was stout with beady eyes which never missed anything.

When Esther was teasing Leyla that she could not hop nearly as far as she could, Mrs Turkey stopped absolutely still, then turned her wrinkled neck to look at Esther – very crossly.

When Leyla was jumping in the puddles and splashing everyone, Mrs Turkey stopped absolutely still, then turned her wrinkled neck to look at Leyla – very crossly indeed.

'I think those beady eyes only know how to look cross,' said Esther as the twins hopped slowly across the yard and into the schoolroom in the barn.

'Or very cross indeed,' added Leyla.

All the other animals were arriving at the same time. Mrs Turkey was sitting in the corner, quietly writing. As each one came in, she turned her wrinkled neck to look at them – very kindly indeed.

'Hello class,' she said with a big smile. 'You all know me, I'm Mrs Turkey. And I think we are going to get on really well.' And do you know, she was right!

Scott the rabbit had a new ball. It was bright red, and it was *very* bouncy. He could not wait to show all his friends how bouncy it was. He bounced it on the ground. It flew up and hit the barn, waking the hen.

'Go and play with your ball somewhere else,' she squawked. 'You woke me up!'

He hopped to the other side of the farmyard and bounced it again. It flew even higher and bounced down on the back of the grumpy old goat.

'Go and play with your ball somewhere else,' he grumbled. 'That hurt!'

'Bother,' said Scott. He took his ball to the edge of the farmyard. This time he bounced it so high that it bounced and bounced and – vanished over the farmyard wall. Scott scurried under the fence and looked around. He could not see his ball anywhere. He hopped a little further and looked round – still no ball.

Then he looked up. He could not believe his eyes! Wherever he looked, the trees were covered in red balls.

'How will I ever find mine?' he wailed. Then Sarah Squirrel's face peered out from between the branches.

'You silly rabbit,' she laughed. 'These are apples! Try looking on the ground.' And, sure enough, that was where Scott found his bright red ball.

GINGER, THE GUARD CAT

Ginger Cat lived on the farm. Every night at bedtime he went round to check that all the animals were safe.

'Silly old Ginger,' said Mrs Hen. 'He thinks he's a guard dog.'

Ginger even visited Boris Bull, who was so fierce he had to live in a field on his own.

One night, Ginger was keeping watch as usual. He went to see Gregory Goat.

'Everything all right?' he asked.

'Yes, thank you.' said Gregory.

He went to visit Mrs Hen in her coop, even though she sometimes made fun of him.

'Everything all right?' he started to ask.

But everything wasn't all right. The lock on the hen house door was broken. Fergus Fox was trying to get in. Ginger ran back to the farmhouse and jumped through the open window.

'Miaow, miaow, miaow,' he said loudly. He woke up the farmer, who chased Fergus Fox away.

'Thank you for saving me and my chicks,' said Mrs Hen. 'You really are as brave as a guard dog.'

And she never made fun of Ginger Cat again.

Corky Cockerel had a very sore throat.

'You must rest your voice,' said David Donkey.

'Tomorrow morning I have to sit on the cowshed roof and crow,' said Corky. 'All the animals depend on me to wake them up.'

'Somebody must do it for you,' said David. So Corky Cockerel's friends lined up to have a try.

Mrs Hen flew on to the cowshed roof and went, 'Cluck, cluck,'

'Not loud enough,' said Corky.

Mrs Goose had a turn.

'Honk, honk,' went Mrs Goose.

'Far too quiet,' said Corky.

Mrs Turkey took her place on the cowshed roof.

'Gobble, gobble,' went Mrs Turkey.

'I can't hear you,' said Corky Cockerel.

Corky was worried. What could he do now?

David Donkey said, 'Let me have a try.'

'You can't climb on the cowshed roof,' said Corky.

But David threw back his head and went, 'Hee-haw, hee-haw.' It was so loud that all the animals heard him, even those in the nearby fields.

'Just think what it would be like if I climbed on the cowshed roof!' said David proudly.

Hop and Skip, the twin white goats, hated bath night. Every time their mother called them in they made hundreds of excuses.

'I can't have a bath tonight,' Hop said. 'I've got my homework to do.'

'I've still got a bandage on my knee where I fell off my bike,' said Skip. 'It will come off in the bath.'

Their mother had had enough of excuses, however, and into the bath they went. As it was a warm summer's evening she said they could go outside to dry off before bed. The bath had made their coats silky and soft.

'Oh, you look lovely,' said Kitty the calf. 'Your fur is so white.'

Tim the turkey waddled over. 'My, my, what a smart pair you are!'

Then Ronald the robin, who lived in an old watering can in the corner of the barn, flew down, crying, 'I've never seen your coats so silky.' Hop and Skip blushed.

'Perhaps bathtime isn't so bad!' they laughed.

Soon it would be Carol the calf's birthday. She wrote invitations to her party and gave them to her friends. She learned a song to sing to them, as a surprise.

Her friends brought her some lovely presents: a paintbox, a book, a box of chocolates and a necklace.

They had tea in the garden – crisps, cherry buns, jam tarts and ice cream. Carol blew out her candles in one big puff. After tea, they played hide and seek and pass the parcel. Then Carol sang her surprise song.

When she'd finished, everybody clapped. Carol's friends had planned some surprises too. Perky did a dance while Christine played her mouth organ. Cuthbert played a tune on his recorder. The others sang a song and the neighbours opened their windows and joined in the chorus.

'Wasn't I lucky, Mum?' Carol said after her friends had gone home. 'I always have a party, but this year was really special. I had a Carol concert!'

I want to fly!' said Marigold to her friend Polly the pig.

'Hens can't fly very far,' said Polly.

'But I want to fly over the moon and over the stars!' said Marigold.

'A cow jumped over the moon once,' mooed Henrietta the cow, thoughtfully.

Marigold flapped her short brown wings but she only managed to flutter up to the lowest branches of a tree.

'If I could get to the top of the tree,' she said, 'and jump off, then I might reach the moon!'

Oliver the cat was sleeping in the branches of the tree.

'Oliver, I want to get to the top,' she said.

'Then climb aboard, my friend,' smiled Oliver. 'I'll take you!'

Marigold reached the top of the tree. 'Oh, deary me!' she said. The ground looked so far away it made her dizzy. But she was determined.

'Wheeeee!' she yelled as she jumped off. She tried to go upwards but . . . down . . . down . . . down she went until . . . Plonk! she landed on Polly's head.

'I don't want a hen as a hat!' giggled Polly.

'Oh deary me!' clucked Marigold. She had lost a few feathers but otherwise only her pride was hurt. 'In future I will stick to the ground!'

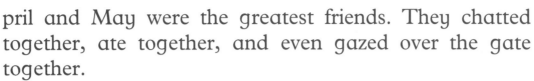

April and May were the greatest friends. They chatted together, ate together, and even gazed over the gate together.

Once, however, they nearly fell out. They were grazing as usual, when suddenly – both together – they spotted something in the grass. It was a lucky four-leaf clover!

'Mine, I think,' said April, picking it up neatly with her teeth.

'I think *not*,' said May angrily. 'I saw it at exactly the same time.'

'Well, it seems as though *I* have it,' said April out of the corner of her mouth.

'Only because you grabbed!' said May. And she was so cross she reached over, and snatched the four-leaf clover with her teeth. April hung on tight – and between them the four-leaf clover was torn in two!

They looked at each other aghast – then suddenly burst out laughing. They both looked so silly.

'Let's not ruin our friendship over one silly little plant,' said May.

'No!' said April. 'We can share the luck between us!'

Dominic, the farmer's son, kept Clover and Nutmeg, his black and white rabbits, in a hutch by the farmhouse. He fed them juicy lettuce, cabbage and dandelion leaves every day, and when he came home from school he let them have a run in a big pen he'd made.

Some wild rabbits lived in a high bank not far away, and one night, when everyone was asleep, they crept up to the hutches.

'Why don't you bite your way through the netting on your hutch and come and live with us?' they said to the black and white rabbits. 'We're not shut in. We're free.'

Clover and Nutmeg looked at each other. 'But we have a warm house with clean straw to lie in,' Clover said. 'Dominic brings us our food, and we have a run every day. I don't think we'd be very good at looking after ourselves.'

'You go back to your burrows and we'll stay here,' said Nutmeg. 'We're very comfortable, thank you!'

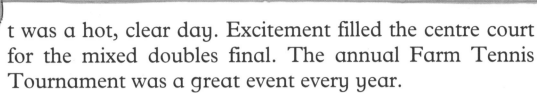

It was a hot, clear day. Excitement filled the centre court for the mixed doubles final. The annual Farm Tennis Tournament was a great event every year.

As Porky the pig and Feather the chicken strode confidently on to the court, the crowd cheered. They were sure to win. Then came Starlight the horse and Denise the cow. Their friends had to cheer especially loudly because there weren't many of them.

'Will the audience go to their seats,' announced Mr Pig. 'The game will begin in five minutes.'

The first set was easy. Porky was famous for his tricks and Feather for her speed. They looked at each other proudly and held their noses in the air. They were sure to win.

But Starlight and Denise soon began to play better. They were enjoying themselves. Porky and Feather began to make mistakes. Porky hit too heavily and the ball flew off the court. Feather hit too lightly and it did not go over the net.

It was a nail-biting finish, but Starlight and Denise were declared the new champions, which just goes to show that no-one is *sure* to win.

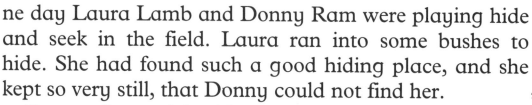

One day Laura Lamb and Donny Ram were playing hide and seek in the field. Laura ran into some bushes to hide. She had found such a good hiding place, and she kept so very still, that Donny could not find her.

'Laura, Laura,' he bleated, but Laura had gone to sleep and did not hear him!

Suddenly, she awoke with a start. Something was tickling her nose. She froze. She did not dare to move. She lay there very, very still and the thing went on tickling her nose.

Meanwhile, Donny had gone to tell the others that Laura was missing. Soon they were all searching.

'Laura, come baaack,' they called.

'Baa, I'm here,' she bleated, keeping as still as she could. Her mother barged through the bushes.

'Whatever are you doing?' she asked.

'I daren't move,' whispered Laura. 'There's something on my nose.' Her mum laughed.

'You silly lamb. It's only a spider making a web. You stayed still for so long she must have thought you were part of the bush. Come on, now. It's time to go home for tea. The spider will have to start again.'

Martha loved to sing. She knew all the songs that played on the radio in the milking shed. But the other cows weren't interested in listening to her. They preferred munching grass all day. Martha needed an audience, so she ambled off around the farm to find someone who would appreciate her talents.

Passing the duck pond she noticed some activity in amongst the reeds. There she found several frogs croaking away to one of her favourite songs, and she started to sing along with them. Martha sang as loud as she could and the frogs joined in with all the choruses. Soon a big crowd of farm animals had gathered around the pond and were clapping along with Martha's performance.

'What's going on?' asked the other cows, who had walked over to see where the noise was coming from.

'It's a new band,' shouted the ducks. 'They are called Martha and the Croakettes!'

THE NOISY ROOSTER

The first animal to wake in the farmyard was always Roland Rooster. The first thing he did was climb onto a haystack, open his beak – and wake everyone else up! His 'cock-a-doodle-doo' was the loudest in the village.

The animals all grumbled about Roland's crowing.

'That noise goes right through me,' said Wilbur Pig.

'It gives me ever such a fright,' said Fiona Foal.

'I was having a lovely dream this morning,' said Sylvia Sheep, 'until Roland's crowing ruined it.'

One day, however, Roland had a sore throat and couldn't crow in the morning. So everyone overslept.

Wilbur was behind all day with his work, the farmer was late with Fiona's oats and, because she slept so late, Sylvia's dream turned into a nightmare!

It didn't take long for the animals to change their mind about Roland.

'I hope your voice gets better soon,' they told him. 'We don't like being woken up so early – but it's better than NOT being woken up at all!'

100

Helen the deer's grandma was coming to stay.

'I'll gather some flowers to put in Grandma's room,' Helen thought.

There were lots of pretty flowers growing in the fields near Helen's home – bluebells, buttercups and daisies. But at the bottom of the field near a stream, she noticed some golden-yellow flowers which looked prettier than all the rest.

'I must have some of those,' Helen thought.

She ran through the long, damp grass to where they were growing. But the ground was so soft and squelchy near the river, that her feet began to sink in the mud. Poor Helen felt very frightened!

As she sank deeper, Helen grabbed at a bush to save herself. Still hanging on, she stretched out and reached the golden flowers and picked a precious few. Then she managed to pull herself out of the mud. She looked an awful mess. But she was very pleased with the flowers.

When she got home she put the flowers in a little jug. They looked so beautiful that she almost forgot how frightened she had felt when she sank in the mud. But when she looked at her feet she remembered! She would not pick those flowers again no matter how beautiful they were. And she rushed off to wash her feet before Grandma arrived.

Mr & Mrs Longneck kept their important things in a very high cupboard in the bathroom where young Leonard Longneck couldn't reach them.

Leonard, being a curious giraffe, wished he could reach the cupboard so that he could see the treasures he imagined lay within.

One day, while his parents were busy in the kitchen, Leonard balanced the clothes basket on top of the bathroom stool and climbed up to peer into the cupboard.

But the door was shut tight!

Leonard pulled and pulled, but the door wouldn't budge. Leonard gave one last tremendous heave, and the door flew open. Leonard fell to the floor with a crash, grazing his knee.

Mrs Longneck rushed in to see Leonard rubbing at his sore knee.

'What on earth have you done?' she asked.

'I wanted to see the treasure in the cupboard,' Leonard replied.

'There's no treasure in there,' sighed Mrs Longneck, reaching into the cupboard and taking out plasters and ointment. 'Just these.' That was lucky for Leonard, since his knee was hurting by this time and the plasters and ointment felt like treasure as they soothed the pain.

It was the night before the Jungle Birds' Choir put on an open-air concert for all the other creatures.

Young Tommy Toucan had to sing a solo. He went to bed early to get plenty of rest, but as he peered out into the darkness, he saw lots of bright lights.

'They're only friendly fireflies!' his mummy said when he called her.

Mummy explained that fireflies were really flying beetles with glowing light-spots on them.

On the night of the concert, the audience began to file in and take their seats by the stage, all chattering noisily. But just as the choir was about to sing the first note, all the stage lights went out.

'Whatever shall we do?' asked Helen Hummingbird.

Tommy Toucan wasn't going to sing in the dark – it was his big night and he wanted to be seen. 'Fetch the fireflies!' he told his mother. And that is just what she did. The Jungle Birds' Choir sang under hundreds of flitting 'spotlights', and everyone agreed that it was their best concert ever.

The little boa constrictors surrounded the large, old snake who was curled up asleep in the hollow of a tree.

'Tell us the story about your jungle journey, Grandpa,' they said, waking him from a pleasant dream.

'It was a long time ago,' he began. 'I set off to find the hidden temple on the other side of the jungle. First I travelled far through the undergrowth towards the rising sun, never stopping for a rest or a snack. As the sun rose high, I changed direction, circling round in great loops to cover my tracks.'

'Who would be following, Grandpa?' asked the smallest boa, but Grandpa didn't stop to answer.

'Finally,' he continued, 'I went up and made my way along the tree branches – up and along, up and along – to give me a view of the way ahead . . .'

The little ones watched with delight as the old snake stopped short – always at the same point in the tale. For as he spoke, he followed the route of his adventure, winding himself round the branches of the tree, stretching and curling until he tied himself into a huge knot! Then the giggling snakes had to untie him and settle him down for a rest! They never did find out if he found the temple, but it was still their favourite story.

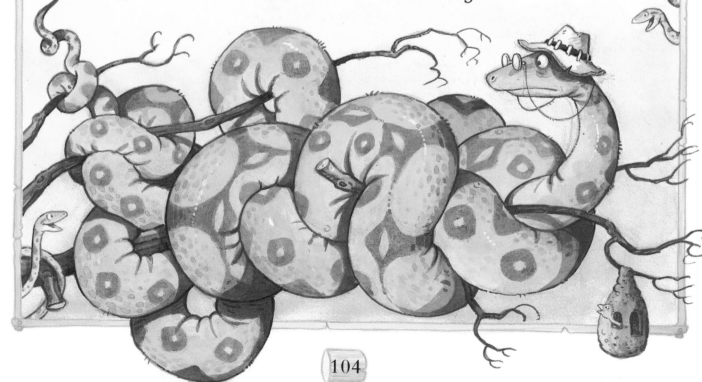

No more complaining,' said Jeremy's mum. 'You keep falling out of the nest. Tonight you can sleep on the ground with the adults.'

'But I don't want to sleep down there,' Jeremy persisted. 'It's not as warm and cosy on the ground.'

'Nonsense,' replied his mother. 'It's very soft.'

'Can't I make my own nest?' begged Jeremy.

'If you want to,' his mum replied doubtfully, 'but you won't be as comfortable.'

Jeremy worked at his high tree nest all afternoon. That night, he snuggled down, wriggling to make himself comfortable.

A twig stuck in his back. A leafy branch poked in his ear. He shuffled again, rocking the nest. And finally, after more wriggling, he fell right out of the nest and into a patch of ferns.

As he began to climb back into the tree, he noticed how soft the ferns were. Without thinking, he pulled a few around him, rested his head on a pile of leaves and drifted quickly back to sleep.

'Did you fall out of your nest last night?' his mum asked with a smile when he woke up next morning.

'Oh no,' said Jeremy. 'I decided I would rather sleep on the ground after all!'

Wally was a boastful monkey. He knew that he was the fastest as they swung between the trees, the bravest when they raced to the treetops, and the most skilful at balancing on the thinnest branches.

'I can go the highest,' boasted Wally one day. 'I can even climb that thin branch.' The monkeys gasped.'You couldn't!' they cried. But Wilma was fed up with Wally's boasting. She had noticed that he had grown fatter since the last race.

'Race you up there!' she said.

The two monkeys sped off up the branches. Quick as a flash, Wally had reached the skinny branch on the tree top. 'I won!' he cried to the others below. But the branch began to crack . . . Wally couldn't climb off in time, and as the branch broke and fell, he tumbled down with it, crashing through leaves and branches. Wilma caught hold of the end of his tail as he fell. 'Ouch!' he cried, as he dangled a few feet above the ground. The monkeys cheered – Wilma had saved his life, and Wally never boasted again.

Whenever anyone wanted to know anything, such as where they had left their keys, or when a birthday was, they only had to ask Albert the elephant. Because Albert, like any elephant, had an amazing memory. He quite simply never forgot.

But one day, Albert did forget. He was just taking a stroll through the jungle, when suddenly, a falling coconut landed on his head. Albert began to see stars . . . Peregrine Monkey saw it happen. He did think it was funny, but he said, 'Albert? Are you all right?'

'Who's Albert?' said Albert the elephant. Poor Albert couldn't even remember his name! He couldn't remember where he lived, what his friends' names were, or even why he had a trunk!

His friends were very worried about him. It was Peregrine who said, 'Well, if a coconut can make him *lose* his memory, perhaps it can help him *find* it again too!'

The animals decided to give it a try. Peregrine climbed a tall tree with a large coconut, and dropped it on Albert's head. Albert was *very* cross. 'Peregrine Monkey!' he cried. 'I could have lost my memory with a blow like that!'

Albert was his old self again!

The animals chattered excitedly one morning as they gathered for school.

'What do you think the new teacher will be like?' they asked, scurrying about, too excited to sit in their places.

'Let's draw a picture of him on the blackboard,' said one of the cheekier monkeys, 'and see if it looks like him!' With an orange chalk, he drew a large, hairy face. His friend filled in a wide, toothy grin and a sagging double chin. The others added a pot-belly, long hairy arms, and huge feet.

The class stood back, giggling, to admire their work, when a low voice made them jump.

'Good morning, children.' The animals gasped and rushed back to their places.

The teacher walked to the front of the class, swaying slightly on his big feet, his long hairy arms hanging beside him and his big pot belly sticking out in front. He looked at the picture and his mouth spread into a wide, toothy grin.

'Well, children,' he said proudly, 'What a fetching portrait of me!'

And the animals knew at once that they would get on well with their new school teacher.

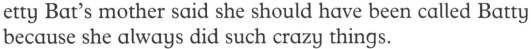

Betty Bat's mother said she should have been called Batty because she always did such crazy things.

Once, Betty decided that she was bored with eating fruit and was going to hunt insects instead. She ended up with a dreadful stomach ache.

Another time, Betty tried sleeping rightside up like other animals, instead of upside down. It was very difficult to balance. She fell off the branch when she was half-asleep, and landed on her head!

It was Betty who hung too near the end of the branch to see if it would hold her weight – and ended up with bruises all over her body when the branch snapped, and she fell to the ground.

So it came as quite a surprise to everyone when Betty announced that she was going to try to be a sensible bat. Then she flew off to find a meal just as the sun was rising above the jungle and all the other bats were just settling down to sleep!

The rain lashed through the trees, huge drops bouncing off the leaves and dripping down to the jungle floor.

The parrots roosted comfortably on the high branches. The leopards and tigers were nowhere to be seen, hiding away until the rainstorm passed. The python was curled snugly in a tree hollow, eyes closed.

But suddenly a whoop of delight and a flurry of activity rocked the python from his slumber and made him curl down his head and flick out his tongue to find out what was going on. There were swishing and splashing sounds, sliding and slurping noises, loud chatterings and giggles.

And what he saw made his snake eyes widen even further. For down below him was a bustle of the brightest and jolliest tree frogs he had ever seen. Amidst hoots of joy, they were sliding down a huge waterchute which they had made by lashing together a spiral of the biggest, most slippery leaves. They slid down, helter-skelter, landing with a tremendous splash in a muddy mess on the jungle floor.

'Children!' sighed the snake, curling back to sleep with a wide yawn. 'I slide down slippery slopes every day, and I never make such a fuss about it!'

The monkey troop had just moved to a new patch of the jungle and the youngsters were exploring.

'Hey, look at this!' cried Jessie to her brother and sister. Growing on a tree trunk, was the largest flower the monkeys had ever seen. It had great brown and white spots, and it smelt TERRIBLE!

Simon grinned wickedly. 'We can use it as a stinkbomb!' And that is what they did. Before long, the whole neighbourhood began to complain about an odd smell. When the chimps got home, Mum said, 'Into the bath with the lot of you! You smell awful!'

The chimps groaned, as Mum scrubbed behind their ears. Of course, even when the children were sparkling clean, the smell didn't go away. 'Hmm,' said Mum. 'Maybe I didn't wash you well enough . . .'

'No!' cried the chimps, and they told her about how they had used the flower as a stinkbomb – anything was better than another bath. Mum was very cross. She made them scrub clean every nest in the street. 'That flower is called a Rafflesia, and you are never to touch it again!' she said.

'We won't!' wailed the chimps, as they polished and scrubbed.

Peter was certainly a friend it was a little hard to get close to. You could nuzzle his nose quite safely, but to approach him from any other angle was not a good idea. For Peter was a porcupine. What's more he was a very large and round porcupine for his age.

He was also a very friendly and helpful chap. If Peter noticed someone struggling with their shopping, he would rush up to help. But so many animals had dropped their bags and parcels in fright, that it rather put him off.

Then Mrs Armadillo came to the rescue. Peter's appearance did not bother her. She hung all her bags from the spikes on his back, and everyone could see how useful he could be.

After that, Peter was never short of people who needed his help. In fact, he was in great demand as the best shopping carrier in the jungle.

The baby crocodiles liked nothing better than to swim in the river, while their mother watched lazily from the bank, or slid into the water for a cooling dip.

Harry was particularly adventurous. In fact, his mother complained that he was too adventurous because he often swam right out into the swift-flowing river and was carried downstream. Then one of the adults had to rescue him and bring him back to safety. They always told him off.

'You are a foolish crocodile,' they nagged. 'One of these days, you'll float off right down the river and never come back.' But he always smiled broadly because it really was such fun!

But one day, he went too far. When he had been rescued for the fourth time, Grandpa, the oldest and the largest crocodile, decided he had had enough. He waded downstream into the river and stuck his great feet into the mud, making a barrier across the water.

'Now you can't go any further,' he said, 'and we can have a rest!'

But do you know, it was just as much fun floating down the current and bumping into Grandpa as it was floating further downstream. So everyone was happy.

W here shall I hide?' David, the little shrew, muttered as he scampered about the undergrowth on the jungle floor. He could hear the others slowly counting up to 50 . . . He had to find a good hiding place.

As he turned round for the umpteenth time, a beautiful bird of paradise flew down and rested on a branch. His magnificent tail cascaded on the ground.

'That's it!' said David, rushing to hide himself.

'Coming!' came the cry, and shrews darted in all directions. The bird looked at David.

'Can I be of any assistance?' he asked.

'Yes, please,' whispered David. 'First they have to find me and then join me in my hiding place. But there's not enough room.'

'Just leave it to me,' said the bird.

Christopher's face popped between the feathers.

'There you are,' he said. 'Not much room here!'

'Allow me!' said the bird of paradise and spread his tail, fan-like, a little further.

'Found you!' cried Melissa. 'Bit of a squeeze!'

'Allow me!' said the bird of paradise, again spreading his tail feathers to hide them perfectly.

By the end of the game, all the shrews were huddled together under the colourful canopy of feathers. What a wonderful game! And everyone said that David's hiding place was the best one ever.

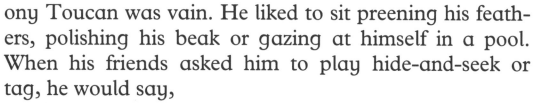

Tony Toucan was vain. He liked to sit preening his feathers, polishing his beak or gazing at himself in a pool. When his friends asked him to play hide-and-seek or tag, he would say,

'No, I might ruffle my feathers.'

One day, Tony's friend Tricia had an idea. There had been a rainstorm and the jungle was muddy and wet.

'Fly down to the river with me,' she said. 'We can stop at every puddle, if you like.' So off they flew, chatting happily. As they flew to the first pool, some mud splashed on Tony's legs, but he was looking at his face, so he didn't notice.

At the second, his wing dipped in the muddy water, but he was admiring his beak so he didn't notice. At the third pool, his face was splattered with mud, but Tricia shouted, 'Oh, look at that wonderful flower,' to distract his attention, and he didn't notice.

Finally they reached the river, but before Tony could look at his reflection, Tricia said,

'Haven't we had a lovely morning?' Tony looked down in surprise at the mud-splattered bird gazing at him from the water, but somehow it didn't matter that he looked a mess.

'Yes,' he said, smiling, 'We have!'

Cedric was a very small flying squirrel with three spots on his left wrist, and two spots on his right wrist. Cedric was a terrible flier and he wished that he could be less clumsy. When the other squirrels leapt out to glide across the air from tree to tree, they landed exactly where they wanted. But Cedric landed with a bump into the tree trunk. The trouble was that Cedric didn't know his right from his left. When his mother shouted, 'Left arm forward!' Cedric moved his right arm. And when she shouted, 'Right leg down!' Cedric moved his left.

'What are we going to do with you?' his mother would say, shaking her head in despair, after a disastrous gliding lesson. Cedric's brother had an idea.

'He can use his spots as a code!' he cried. Of course, Cedric had no trouble remembering his spots. 'Three spots forward!' meant his left arm, and 'Two spots back!' meant his right. After that, it was all plain sailing.

It was the middle of the day, the sun was shining, and Brenda the bushbaby couldn't sleep.

'It always sounds so exciting in the jungle in the day-time,' she thought. 'Why do we bushbabies miss all the fun by sleeping in the day and coming out at night?' Brenda was curious. Carefully, so that she did not wake the family, Brenda climbed out of the nest.

A snuffling and scurrying in the undergrowth made her jump. It was a large bony armadillo wandering past. A loud screeching sound and a great flapping of wings startled her and made her cling tightly to the tree. It was a family of brightly-coloured parrots flying by. A rocking of the branches and a chittering and chattering sent her rushing back towards the hole. It was a troop of mischievous monkeys playing games. Brenda climbed quickly back into the hole and snuggled down again next to her mother.

'I think it is much too exciting in the jungle in the day-time,' she said as she went back to sleep. 'I'll come out again at night.'

The sloth family had decided to go on an outing. In fact, it took them all week to decide to go on an outing, because it took them so long to do *anything*.

The morning of the outing arrived, and the family lazily began to gather in the branches.

'I'll just have a look around,' Dad said, 'to make sure it's a good day to go.' He set off, moving his hands in slow motion as he hung under the branch. The others waited patiently, munching slowly on a leaf, swaying and dozing a little as they hung there. They were in no hurry. Finally, Dad returned.

'It's a good day for an outing,' he announced. 'Now which way were we going to go?'

This caused a problem, for none of them could remember. As it reached mid-day and they began to get hungry, they decided to eat lunch before setting off.

After lunch, they thought they'd have a little nap. They spread out in the tree and dozed happily in the warmth. By the time they woke up, the sun was beginning to drop in the sky.

'It's a bit late to set off now,' said Dad. 'Perhaps we had better go another day.'

'We can think about it tomorrow,' said Mum.

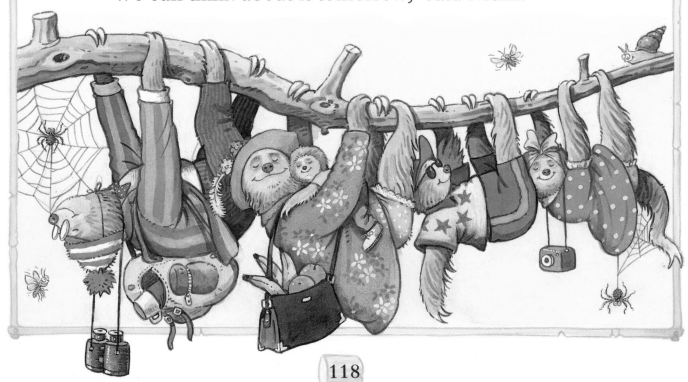

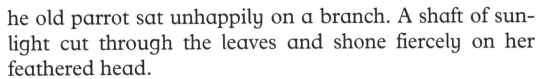

The old parrot sat unhappily on a branch. A shaft of sunlight cut through the leaves and shone fiercely on her feathered head.

'It's too hot,' she squawked, and shuffled along the branch back into the shade.

'Not feeling well today, Rosie?' asked Sam, a bright blue and red parrot, flying over to land on the branch. 'You look very dull in the feathers.'

As the leaves moved, another ray of sun shone brightly on Rosie's curved beak. She squinted and moved again along the branch.

'No,' she murmured sadly. 'I'm all hot and bothered.'

'I'll soon have you sorted out,' said Sam.

Sam flew off and when he returned, he was followed by a flock of tiny hummingbirds. Rosie was mystified, but only for a moment. The hummingbirds flew around her and hovered in a circle. Humming quietly, the rapid beats of their wings fanned cool air all around Rosie and made her feel cooler for the first time that day.

'Oh, Sam, what an excellent idea,' said Rosie. 'Now I know I shall feel better in no time.'

One year Little Tusker Elephant decided to spend the summer living by the river at the edge of the jungle. He built himself a cosy house and then looked round for a few friends. Everyone likes friends to chat to.

However most of the other creatures seemed rather afraid of him and ran away when he came thud-thud-thudding along on his big, round feet.

Then one day, a deer noticed Little Tusker sucking water up from the river and squirting it over his back.

'That's a very useful thing to be able to do,' she said. 'Would you squirt water over my youngsters for me, please? They certainly need cleaning.'

Little Tusker was happy to give the young deer a wash. And they loved the water squiggling all over them. Word spread and soon lots of the animals were coming for a shower and of course a gossip. Before long, Little Tusker had lots of friends. Knowing how to do something useful is a good way to get to know people.

Rainbow sat on a branch, feeling lonely. He swivelled his eyes around and caught sight of his uncle resting in the leaves above him.

'Hello, Uncle,' said Rainbow, climbing up to him. 'There are lots of flies by that big flower on the jungle floor. Come down and have lunch with me.'

'Not hungry, son,' muttered his uncle, and slithered away. His cousin Charlie was standing by a flower so Rainbow made his way down to join him.

'Hello, Charlie,' said Rainbow happily. 'Mind if I share your lunch?'

'I prefer to eat alone,' Charlie grunted.

Rainbow knew when he was not wanted. He walked off sadly. Then he heard a rustle and a sniff. A frog was sitting in a puddle on a leaf.

'Hello,' said Rainbow. 'You look down in the mouth.' The frog gulped loudly.

'I'm not like the other frogs,' he complained. 'They are happy on their own but I want someone to talk to.'

'Why, so do I!' said Rainbow happily. 'Where do you come from? Would you like some lunch? What's your name, by the way?' And the pair walked happily off, chatting about this, that and five dozen other things to their hearts' content.

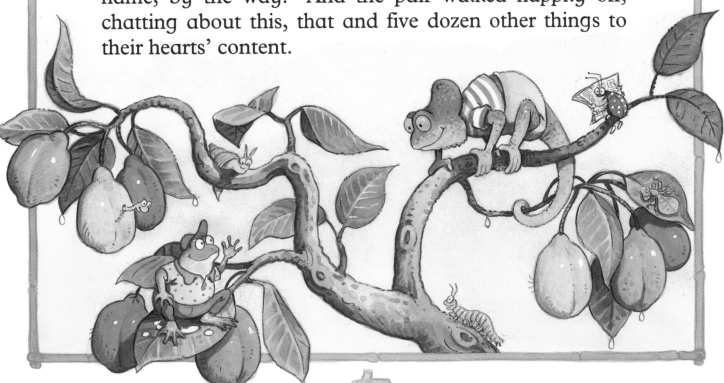

Thomas played happily on the bank of the river chasing butterflies while the rest of his family lazed along the banks, keeping cool in the lapping water.

'Come and cool down,' said his dad. 'It's lovely.' But Thomas would not set foot in the river. Unlike all the other tigers, he hated the water.

Just then, Thomas spotted the biggest, most brightly coloured butterfly he had ever seen. He leapt in the air, batting at it with his paws. The butterfly darted this way and that with Thomas following behind.

He was concentrating so hard on the butterfly that he did not notice when his back paws dipped into the water as he ran along, and his tail swished great splashes into the air; or when he landed with a great splosh in the shallows after an especially high leap. When the little butterfly fluttered away from the river Thomas was wet from nose to tail.

'You can hardly say you don't like the water now,' said his dad. Thomas looked at himself – covered in glistening drops.

'Isn't it nice and cool in the river?' his dad laughed.

The parrots had wings and could fly anywhere. Sometimes, they flew for miles to explore the jungle and still came back in time for tea.

Old Grandma Parrot had explored wondrous lands in her day. She had a good memory as well. When any of the little monkeys could not get to sleep at night, Mummy Monkey used to send for Grandma Parrot to tell them a story. Their favourite stories were about her adventures at sea when she sailed with pirates and perched on the Captain's shoulder.

'We used to have fights at sea in our sailing ships,' squawked Grandma Parrot. 'We stole chests full of gold and buried them on a desert island, marking the place with a cross.'

'Is it still there? Will you show us how to find it?' the little monkeys would ask.

But Grandma Parrot would just laugh. 'When you are grown up and can fly, I will,' she said.

Of course the little monkeys never did learn to fly even though they practised every day, and the treasure is probably there still, waiting to be found.

Slinky the snake liked living in the jungle. He never bothered to go to school. He thought school was no fun at all. What was fun was slithering up and down trees all day. The best game was crawling to the end of a branch where it was as thin as could be and hanging there, swinging in the wind. But one day Slinky went on to a branch that was too thin, or Slinky was too fat. Whichever it was, the branch broke and Slinky fell down, down, down into the muddy river.

Slinky couldn't swim. He coughed and choked, struggled and wriggled and at last climbed out of the river.

How the other animals laughed!

Now if only Slinky had bothered to go to school, he might have learned how to swim.

My favourite spot is down by the edge of a little waterhole 'I know,' said Walter Warthog. 'Then I can enjoy a nice mud-bath!'

'Ooh! It sounds very sticky!' replied Cherry Chimp. 'My favourite spot is up in a big, shady tree!'

Soon some other animals arrived and each of them thought of their favourite spot.

'Mine is among some lush grass, by the river,' said Brett Buffalo dreamily.

'I know a nice rocky spot where I can sit and see for miles,' said Bessie Baboon.

So it went on as, one after another, the animals spoke up. When it came to Oscar Ostrich's turn, he looked quite puzzled. 'The trouble is I have lots of favourite spots,' he said.

'Where are they?' asked Walter.

The others waited for Oscar to answer. Suddenly, he pointed to someone running to join them.

'Here they come now!' replied Oscar. 'See? They're on Chas Cheetah's fur. They must be my favourite spots because he's my favourite friend!'

THE OBSTACLE RACE

The jungle was buzzing with excitement as the day of the obstacle race approached. The young gibbons always tried to find out what the race had in store, but they never succeeded.

'We have one last chance to sneak a look!' Monty whispered to his friends. 'And I have a plan.' He had made a cloak of leaves which he threw over his head. 'They'll never spot me in this disguise,' he boasted as he set off. The trouble was it was rather difficult to see out of the leafy cloak, and rather difficult to tread quietly when he couldn't see where he was going. When he could almost see the obstacle course, one of the sentries slowly swung towards him.

'Look, George,' he called to a friend, 'here's a nice bunch of leaves. Let's stop for a break.' With a sly wink, the two sat next to Monty and began picking leaves from his cloak. Poor Monty sat frozen to the spot as his disguise slowly disappeared. Finally, George lifted the leaf that hid Monty's face.

'Why, Monty!' he cried in pretended surprise. 'What on earth are you doing here?' Monty did not wait to answer; he fled. The two old gibbons laughed.

'I could have told him that trick wouldn't work,' laughed George. 'I tried it when I was his age!'

Lizzie Leopard had a skipping-rope. She practised with it until she could skip forwards, backwards, do double-skips and even triple-skips!

One afternoon, Rory Rhinoceros saw her.

'I wish I could skip,' he sighed.

'I'll teach you!' replied Lizzie.

Rory borrowed the skipping-rope and started to skip. THUD-KER-THUD! THUMPETY-THUD!

Lizzie had forgotten how very heavy Rory was. As he jumped up and down, the ground shook so much that Lizzie's dad bounced out of his garden chair.

Indoors, things fell off shelves and tables and the whole house vibrated.

'Stop!' Lizzie's mum called to Rory from the window, but he did not hear. Then the skipping-rope caught on his foot and Rory tumbled to the ground with one last KER-THUD!

'I think that's enough practice for now,' said Lizzie.

A few days later, Rory passed her home again.

'Can I have another go with your skipping-rope, please?' he asked.

Lizzie led Rory into the back garden to show him her new trampoline.

'Why not use that instead?' she smiled. 'With luck, this time, nothing else will bounce about but you!'

THE JUST RIGHT HOUSE

The Monkey family lived in a cosy house Grandpa and Grandma had built, three quarters of the way up a very tall tree.

'This house is in just the right place,' they said. 'Just high enough to be safe from dangerous leopards, and low enough to be sheltered from the wind.'

But the young monkeys wanted to live where they could see the sky. They built themselves another house at the top of the tree.

'When I was a little chap, my great grandpa told me that once there was such a strong wind that it blew away all the houses at the tops of the trees,' said Grandpa.

The young monkeys laughed and said that strong winds like that did not blow any more – if ever they had!

But one day, a strong wind did blow. It blew the new house to pieces and the young monkeys were glad to climb down to the Just Right House, all safe and sound three quarters of the way up a very tall tree.

Mary Monkey was getting worried. She was looking for her naughty little baby, Maurice, and she couldn't see him anywhere.

'Cooee! Maurice!' she cried, swinging through the tall branches of the trees. 'Come and have some of this delicious fruit I've picked.'

But there was no sign of Maurice anywhere. He wasn't climbing the creepers, or splashing in the waterfall, or teasing the grumpy old toucan. Mary asked everyone she met if they'd seen him, from the squirrels and the parrots up in the trees to the lizards and frogs in the river below. Everyone said no, but they all seemed to be laughing at her, and Mary couldn't understand why.

She soon found out, though.

'Fooled you!' giggled a voice in her ear. 'I've been on your back all the time.'

'Maurice,' said his mother, 'one more trick like that and I'm feeding you to the tigers!'

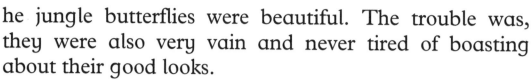

The jungle butterflies were beautiful. The trouble was, they were also very vain and never tired of boasting about their good looks.

'We are so lucky to be colourful,' the butterflies would say as they flitted from flower to flower. 'What a shame you are so plain and dull,' they would say to the elephants and monkeys.

The other animals got tired of listening to them. Then, little Fluffy, the baby elephant, had an idea.

'The water in the pool is so still you can see your reflection in it,' he told the butterflies. 'Why don't you come and look?'

The butterflies flitted across the water admiring their reflection, and it wasn't long before they came just a little bit too close to the water. Once their wings were wet they found they couldn't fly. One after another, they fell into the water with a splash. The monkeys and elephants laughed as they fished out the coughing butterflies, and as for the butterflies – they kept very quiet about their beauty after that!

Tessa Tiger passed along the path to the jungle super-store. She carried a bag and a shopping list which she was reading on the way.

Suddenly, Tessa stepped on a banana skin and slipped over. In the trees above, some monkeys were munching bananas and dropping the skins.

'You should keep the jungle tidy,' called Tessa, angrily, 'and pick up anything that's dropped!'

Tessa collected the banana skins and put them in the litter-bin.

When Tessa got home from the store, she saw with dismay that her bag had a hole in it and all the fruit she had bought had dropped out on the way home! Tessa ran back along the path to find it, and saw the monkeys guzzling her shopping!

'That's my fruit!' she cried.

'Oh sorry,' replied the cheeky monkeys. 'We were just keeping the jungle tidy by picking up anything that's dropped!' And they chuckled as Tessa set off for the store for the second time that day.

Baby Monkey clung to Mummy Monkey's back as she swung through the tree-tops. To such a young monkey, the jungle seemed very big and full of mysterious noises.

'Squawwwk!' came a shrill cry which startled him.

'What's that, M . . . Mummy? ' he asked nervously, holding on to her even more tightly than before.

'Why, it's only Peter Parrot, dear,' she said, pointing as he flew past.

'Pararrrrp!' came another loud noise from somewhere far below.

'What's that, Mummy?' asked Baby Monkey again.

'Only Mister Elephant trumpeting with his trunk.' Mummy Monkey reassured him.

Next moment, a roar made Baby Monkey shiver. Before he could question his mummy about it, she rested on a branch and told him.

'That's Mister Lion calling!' she explained.

'It will take me a long time to learn so many sounds!' chattered Baby Monkey, anxiously. Then he was surprised to hear one he knew straightaway.

'That's Hilda Hyena laughing,' said Mummy Monkey.

'That's the best sound!' giggled Baby Monkey, happily.

One morning, while Ned was breakfasting on a delicious green fern tree, he noticed a huge red and yellow parrot with a long orange beak staring down at him from the top branch.

'Very good morning to you!' said Ned, cheerily. 'What's your name?'

The parrot yelled with laughter and then said, 'I'm not going to talk to *you*. You're just a tiny caterpillar and all you can do is eat.'

Poor Ned was lost for words. He had never met such an unfriendly parrot, and he told his friends Charlie and Harry how mean the parrot had been to him.

That night, when the sky was pitch black, the three caterpillars crept to the fern tree. The parrot was fast asleep on a branch. Ned, Charlie and Harry began to eat all around the branch. They ate and ate and ate until they couldn't swallow another mouthful. At last, the branch broke, and the parrot fell down down to the ground and landed with a bump and a loud screech that woke the whole jungle. The trouble was that Ned felt far too ill to laugh!

There it is again!' shouted Ferdie the Frog to his friend Liza Lizard. 'The wonderful silver ball I keep trying to catch!' And he dived into the water with a spring of his green legs.

'That's no ball,' replied Liza, darting away to her warm cave.

'That's no ball,' hissed a striped snake, slithering through the undergrowth.

'That's no ball,' chattered a troupe of monkeys, swinging home through the trees.

'That's . . . no . . . ball,' droned the sloth, hanging from a tree branch. 'That's . . . the . . . moon!'

But Ferdie was chasing silver splinters all over the pool and didn't hear him. 'I'll get it one day, Liza,' he said. 'You just wait and see!'

I'm so bored,' yawned the quick green lizard. 'I've been sitting on this rock and catching flies all my life. Time for a change!'

So he set off into the jungle to see how other animals lived. First, he tried hanging on a tree branch with the three-toed sloths, but he kept falling off. Then he thought he'd swing through the trees with the monkeys, but they chattered angrily at him and pelted him with nuts. Last of all, he tried hunting with the great stripey tigers. It was dreadful! The whole earth trembled with their fearful roars, and he was almost trodden underfoot by their great paws.

The quick green lizard wanted to return to his old way of life, sitting on a rock and catching flies. 'About time too!' said his mother when she saw him coming home.

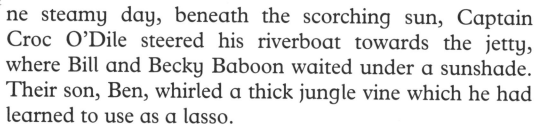

One steamy day, beneath the scorching sun, Captain Croc O'Dile steered his riverboat towards the jetty, where Bill and Becky Baboon waited under a sunshade. Their son, Ben, whirled a thick jungle vine which he had learned to use as a lasso.

'All aboard for a gentle river trip!' cried Captain Croc O'Dile with a lazy smile.

The baboons excitedly climbed aboard but as soon as the boat had set off again, the engine failed. The boat began to drift away in the mangrove swamp . . .

'What shall we do?' they wailed. Just then, Ricky Rhinoceros passed by on the river bank, and Ben had a very clever idea . . . Using his lasso, he quickly cast its loop over the big horn on Ricky's nose, and tied the other end of the lasso to the boat. Ricky towed the riverboat back to the jetty.

'It's lucky you're so strong, Ricky!' said Ben.

'Lucky you're such an expert with a lasso!' replied Ricky, untying the loop from his horn.

'And even luckier Ben kept a cool head on such a hot day!' laughed Captain Croc O'Dile, mooring the riverboat firmly to the jetty.

Auntie Ellie was reading a story to little Edward Elephant and his friends.

'It was the dry season and the jungle waterhole was beginning to dry up . . .' she read.

'Oh! Then how did all the animals bathe?' asked Edward, sitting on her lap.

'I'll tell you later,' replied Auntie Ellie.

'It's such a fine afternoon, you should all go and play for a while.'

The youngsters agreed. Soon they were rushing happily about, playing tag, until they became very hot.

'Phew! Will you read us the rest of that story now while we cool down, please?' Edward asked Auntie Ellie.

'I've a better idea,' she said.

She told all the youngsters to put on their bathing-costumes. Then she walked to the water-hole and filled her long trunk. Hurrying back, she curled her trunk upwards and blew hard. The water sprayed out high into the air, in a great fountain and soaked the youngsters standing underneath.

'I'm glad our water-hole is full,' smiled Auntie Ellie.

'So are we!' laughed Edward.

Jack Crocodile met Harry Zebra on his way to school.

'We get the results of our maths test today,' said Harry, anxiously.

'Oh, I'm not worried,' laughed Jack. 'I always pass – one way or another.'

But when they got to school, their teacher was very cross. 'Everyone has passed the test except for Jack Crocodile. You are a very lazy animal, Jack – that is why you have failed!' she said, sternly.

'Oh dear,' said Jack, trying hard to look sad. Then, Jack yawned loudly at her, opening his mouth very wide indeed.

The teacher looked down his huge throat, with its hundreds of big, sharp teeth, and shivered in her shoes. 'Perhaps I made a mistake!' she cried. 'Why, I think you have passed after all. Well done, Jack!'

Jack leaned back happily in his chair, with a lazy stretch. 'School is so easy if you're a crocodile,' he said to himself.

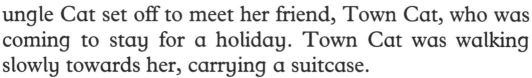

Jungle Cat set off to meet her friend, Town Cat, who was coming to stay for a holiday. Town Cat was walking slowly towards her, carrying a suitcase.

'It's a very long way to the jungle!' sighed Town Cat, wiping her brow with her paw.

'You'll feel better for a rest,' smiled Jungle Cat.

'Phew! It's very hot in the jungle!' gasped Town Cat.

'You'll soon get used to it,' replied Jungle Cat, taking her friend's suitcase.

Town Cat stared at the dense jungle all around.

'The jungle's very big, too!' she said, nervously.

At last, they reached Jungle Cat's home.

'The grass is very tall around here,' said Town Cat. 'I suppose you don't have to cut it once a week with a lawnmower, like I do back home!'

Jungle Cat smiled and, putting down the suitcase indoors, fetched her friend some home-baked banana cookies and coconut-milk shake.

Town Cat thought they tasted delicious. When she had finished them, she wiped her whiskers happily. 'M'm! It's very nice in the jungle, after all,' she said, settling back for a cat-nap in her friend's hammock.

The lion lifted his head, shook his shaggy mane and roared at the top of his voice. He made such a loud noise that a monkey dropped right out of the tree next to him with fright.

'It's still not loud enough to scare me,' said a little mouse who sat on the leaf of a palm tree next to the lion.

'What do you mean?' thundered the lion. 'That's the loudest I've ever roared. Even my father, who was a champion at roaring, couldn't make that much noise.'

'Well, I'm not scared,' said the little mouse. 'You'll have to try harder. I bet I could make a noise that would scare you.'

'Don't be ridiculous, stupid mouse,' said the lion. 'No one in the whole jungle can do that.'

'We'll see about that,' said the little mouse huffily.

The mouse drew in his breath and with all his effort he squealed at the top of his voice. The squeal was so high that human beings could not have heard it, but the lion did. It hurt his ears so much that he turned around and ran off as fast as he could through the jungle.

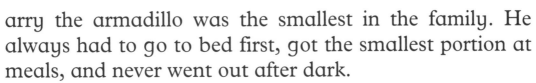

Harry the armadillo was the smallest in the family. He always had to go to bed first, got the smallest portion at meals, and never went out after dark.

'I wonder what it feels like to be a big adventurer,' he thought. 'I think it's about time I found out.' That afternoon he packed a bag with something to eat and set off into the jungle.

'I shall travel to the end of the world!' he announced proudly. He rustled off through the undergrowth until the path forked. Which way should he go? He would stop for an ant snack while he decided.

The hot sun shone down brilliantly and Harry closed his eyes. He felt tired – he must have been walking for almost half an hour! He lay down for a rest and before he knew it, he drifted off to sleep.

Harry woke with a shiver. It was beginning to get dark. What was he doing in this strange place? He must be at the end of the world!

'I don't think I like it,' he said, snuffling round to find his way back along the path.

When he was almost home, he could hear his mother and father calling him.

'Here I am. I've been to the end of the world.'

'Have you indeed?' replied his mum with surprise. 'Well'it's a good thing you came back by bedtime!'

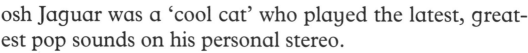

Josh Jaguar was a 'cool cat' who played the latest, greatest pop sounds on his personal stereo.

But his pride and joy was his big, bright juke-box which he had bought at a junk shop and gradually repaired so it worked perfectly.

Every time Josh pressed a different button on it, the juke-box played a golden-oldie rock-and-roll record.

One morning, Annie Ant-eater was heading back from her dance class when she heard Josh's juke-box. Annie had an idea.

'Let's have a party!' she said and Josh agreed.

They invited lots of friends and as the juke-box played everyone danced and danced.

Only when they had played every last record in the juke-box did Josh, Annie and the others sit down to rest.

'What a great time we've had,' said Josh.

'But I'm glad we've run out of records!' puffed Annie.

Josh noticed the crimson sun rising behind the jungle as dawn approached. 'We've been dancing all night!' he chuckled. 'That must be a record, too!'

The animals in the jungle were playing hide and seek. The snake with green and brown scales on his slippery skin thought he would find it easy to hide. He slithered up a tree and pretended to be a branch, but however hard he tried he still didn't look straight and the giraffe spotted him.

'Found you!' she cried. 'Come on. Now you have to find Henrietta the Hippo with me.'

Henrietta was easy to find. Her bottom was so big that no matter where she hid, it stuck out! They discovered her straightaway and together they set off to find Camilla the Chameleon.

Hide and seek was Camilla's favourite game. She had a special gift for changing her colour wherever she stood. First, she stood on a leaf and became green. Next, she jumped down on the earth and became brown. As they walked by, she jumped onto the giraffe's back and her skin took on a black and yellow pattern.

Her friends searched high and low all afternoon, but at last they gave up. 'I'm the winner!' Camilla cried from behind the giraffe's ear, but the animals never wanted to play that game again!

Look at my jungle fan,' boasted Gregory Gorilla to his friends. He was always making machines that were supposed to be helpful. The trouble was, they usually went horribly wrong!

Gregory proudly held up a bamboo pole, with a motor tied to it. He had fixed some large palm leaves on the top of the pole.

'The jungle is boiling hot,' said Gregory, in front of a growing crowd, 'but with my jungle fan, you can be as cool as a cucumber.'

To demonstrate, Gregory flicked the 'on' switch. The motor made the big leaves spin slowly to create a balmy breeze. Gregory was so pleased to see his new machine work that he turned the motor onto full-power. The fan went faster and faster. Suddenly, it took off into the air, taking Gregory with it!

'Help!' he cried, as he began to rise into the tree-tops. His friends managed to catch Gregory's feet and pull him down with a bump. But the fan carried on rising, until it was quite out of sight.

'My fan isn't much use now,' Gregory told his laughing friends, 'but you are all fan-tastic!'

Oliver the Orang-utan sat preening himself in front of the mirror. He was very proud of his beautiful orange hair and often sat and brushed it until it glowed.

His wife looked over as she was cooking their evening supper of baked palm leaves with coconut sauce, and sighed. 'You'll brush all your hair away if you're not careful,' she said.

Oliver scoffed. 'Don't be silly, dear,' he replied. 'Besides, I want to look my best if we're going out swinging later.'

His wife decided to play a trick on him . . . After dinner, Oliver decided to give his hair one last brush before they went out.

But Mrs Orang-utan had collected some orange thread. As Oliver stood brushing his hair, she dropped the pieces of thread all round his feet. When Oliver looked down, he cried, 'My beautiful hair is falling out!' But Mrs Orang-utan only laughed.

'Well, that will teach you not to spend so much time preening yourself,' she said. And it certainly did!

THE BRIGHTEST BIRD

I'm glad I have such bright red feathers!' Red Bird said as he settled on a branch high above the jungle floor.

'My brilliant green feathers sparkle in the sun,' replied Green Bird, perched beside him.

Soon some friends flew down to join them. There were birds in every colour of the rainbow from flame-orange to mauve. They chattered and preened themselves, proudly showing off their wonderful feathers.

Shortly, another bird arrived. Her feathers were dull grey. The others hardly seemed to notice Grey Bird as they chattered and cooed.

Suddenly, Grey Bird spotted dark clouds sweeping across the sky towards them. She flapped her wings and squawked loudly to warn the others.

'A storm is coming. Quickly, find shelter!' sang Grey Bird above the chattering.

Minutes later, savage winds and rain lashed the jungle but, thanks to Grey Bird, everyone watched safely from their nests.

'You're very clever to have warned us about the storm,' Red Bird told her when it had passed. The others agreed.

'Perhaps Grey Bird is the brightest of us all!' smiled Green Bird.

Gina Gorilla liked weaving with jungle grasses. She made a bag for Brenda Baboon, a sun hat for Jim Giraffe, but best of all, she made an enormous hammock for Harry Hippopotamus.

He eagerly tied it between two trees. The hammock was very strong and did not break when hefty Harry climbed into it. But the trees began to bend over. The hammock slowly sank to the ground. When he climbed out, the tree-trunks straightened up again.

'I'm too heavy for a hammock,' sighed Harry.

'It's a shame not to use it,' replied Gina.

Then Harry spotted four young animals fighting over the swing in Owen Ostrich's garden. He had an idea. 'Want a go in my hammock?' he asked the youngsters.

'That's boring!' they cried. 'We're not even sleepy.'

But they didn't think it was boring when Harry persuaded them all to climb in. He pushed them as hard and as fast as he could, so that they went flying through the tree-tops and down again, whooping with delight. 'Now they can all enjoy a swing at the same time!' said Harry, who was just as glad *not* to be scraping about on the ground in his hammock.

Deep in the sun-soaked jungle, a family of snakes was eagerly awaiting Aunt Polly Python's visit. The smallest snake wriggled with excitement while his sister and two older brothers kept slithering up and down a tree to see if their aunt could be seen.

'No sign of her yet!' called one.

'I'm getting tired!' replied another.

'We all are,' smiled Mummy snake. 'Let's take a little nap so we don't feel tired when Aunt Polly gets here.'

'Ho-hum! Good idea,' yawned Daddy snake.

'But if we're all asleep, there'll be no one to greet Aunt Polly,' cried the smallest snake.

Mummy smiled and told everyone exactly how to lie down. When Aunt Polly finally arrived, she looked very carefully at the sleeping snakes and laughed.

'Snakes alive!' Aunt Polly hissed happily. 'Whoever would have thought of such a clever way to give me a warm welcome, without even uttering a sound!'

Mummy snake had made her family shape themselves into letters, to spell the word 'hello'.

What a sensible snake she was!

One afternoon, Professor Trumpetytrunk saw some monkeys playing with a balloon.

'Great elephant's ears!' he gasped. 'That's given me an idea!'

The professor hurried to his jungle workshop and made an enormous balloon out of some of his old socks, (which of course, were very large). He tied his huge armchair to the underside of the balloon.

'My balloon will carry me high above the jungle,' he told the monkeys the next day. 'All I have to do now is to blow up the balloon!'

The professor closed his eyes and puffed into the balloon through his trunk as hard as he possibly could. The monkeys stared as the balloon grew bigger and bigger.

'It's ready!' cried the monkeys. But the professor was puffing so hard that he didn't hear, and the balloon just carried on growing . . . BANG! went the burst balloon, blowing Professor Trumpetytrunk into the sky *without* the help of his balloon.

When the professor came down to earth again with a bump, he cried, 'Great elephant's ears! That's given me another idea!' and the monkeys sighed . . .

Every year, the leopards held a big race to see who was the fastest hunter. 'Ready, Steady, Go!' shouted the old leopard croakily.

The young leopards sprung off to a good start. There were five of them in the race. 'You'll never beat me,' panted Lenny to his neighbour as they ran.

'I've got as good a chance as you do,' said his competitor, Leo.

'Not anymore,' said Lenny as he stuck out his front paw and tripped Leo up. Lenny managed to knock all but one of the young leopards out of the race. He was determined to win.

'Owww,' he yelped suddenly. 'Help!' He had not bargained for getting a thorn stuck in his paw. He dropped to his knees and the last leopard sprinted past him to win the race. The crowd cheered loudly, and no one went to help Lenny. He sat and licked his wounds all on his own, and promised himself that next year he would try to win the race fairly.

Today was a very special day because Merrypen the lion, Lucy the hippopotamus and Julia the Giraffe were going to Benjamin's birthday party. Benjamin was a tiger and today he was seven years old. He had told his friends to dress in their most colourful finery.

Benjamin greeted his guests in his black sunglasses. (Black was Benjamin's favourite colour). Merrypen, Lucy and Julia gave him a black baseball cap and two pairs of black socks – one pair for his front paws and one pair for his back paws.

Benjamin began to try on all his new presents while his friends greedily tucked into the feast that he had made for them. Julia ate the yellow jelly which she kept dropping down her socks before she could reach her mouth. Lucy got her head stuck in the ice-cream bowl, and Merrypen got quite drunk on the lemonade punch which he wouldn't share with anyone.

As for Benjamin, he didn't eat anything at all, because he was such a cool cat that he didn't want to mess up his new outfit. All in all, the birthday party was a great success!

Zola the gibbon lived in a safari park. She and her friends never missed the chance to tease the park-keeper whenever they could. One day, Zola was playing with some of her friends.

'Look at this,' cried George the gazelle. 'The park-keeper has been painting this old wooden fence.'

'Well, I think plain black is a bit boring,' said Zola. 'Let's brighten it up by painting some pictures on it.'

'What a good idea,' said George excitedly. 'Can I paint the first picture?'

George had only just begun to paint when the park-keeper came out of his hut.

Colin the crocodile, in his fright, turned around so quickly that his tail knocked George against the newly painted fence. Colin and Zola took to their heels, leaving George behind.

'You naughty zebra!' shouted the park-keeper at George. 'Just you wait 'til I catch you!'

It wasn't until George caught up with his friends that they realized why the park-keeper had thought he was a zebra – George was covered in black stripes from falling against the fence.

'Well, he'll never catch the mystery zebra now!' Zola laughed, mischievously.

Mum asked Benny the tiger to climb the ladder which led to the loft, so that he could bring her the box of Christmas tree decorations.

'What does the box look like, Mum?' shouted Benny. 'This loft is full of boxes, and they are all covered in dust and the dust is making me sneeze . . .'

No sooner had Benny finished shouting, he felt a VERY BIG sneeze coming on.

He screwed up his wet nose, he covered his face with his paws, he even curled his tail into a knot. But it was no good. Once a sneeze decides to sneeze, not even a Bengal tiger can stop it.

It started with a tickle, then a stinging sensation right in the back of his nose. Finally, the sneeze came. It was fierce and loud and made the whole tiger den shake.

'Are you all right, Benny?' his mother cried, rushing up the loft ladder. 'What was that frightening noise?'

'It's OK, Mum. I only sneezed,' said Benny.

'Have you found the Christmas decorations yet?'

And sure enough he had. For the box of tinsel and baubles had fallen on Benny's head when he sneezed.

Freddie the fruit bat was hanging under a high branch all by himself when Guy the gibbon came swinging by.

'What's the matter with you?' asked Guy. 'You look down in the dumps.'

Freddie sighed. 'I'm fed up,' he said. 'All the other bats are night fliers but I hate flying in the dark – I can't see where I'm going. I'm a day bat and all my friends are asleep during the day, so I've got no one to play with. I even have to eat my tea by myself.'

'What do you eat for tea?' asked Guy.

'Well,' said Freddie, 'I like to eat all sorts of fruits, but bananas are my favourites.'

'I love bananas!' exclaimed Guy. 'Why don't you come back with me and have tea with my family?'

And from that moment on, while the other bats were flying about in the middle of the night, Freddie was fast asleep; and when the bats finally went to bed, Freddie was just waking up, ready for a breakfast of banana sandwiches with his new friend Guy. And he never felt lonely again.

Jim heard laughter as he walked through the forest. 'I wonder who that is?' he thought to himself.

Just then, three animals jumped out in front of him, laughing. 'We've been playing hide and seek,' said one of them. 'But we need a seeker. Would you like to play?'

'Yes, please,' said Jim. He closed his eyes and counted to twenty. When he opened them again, the animals had all gone.

Jim looked up and down, high and low, but he couldn't find any of them. 'I give in,' he said. 'Please come out now.'

Sammy the Snake uncurled himself from the base of the tree. Peter the panther stood up from a dark rock he had been sitting on, and Paula the Parrot flew high into the sky above their heads from the brightly-coloured bush in which she had been hiding.

'Aren't we clever?' they boasted. 'We won easily! You're not very good at seeking'

But Jim just said, 'It's my turn now!' And before the animals had counted to three, Jim the chameleon had completely vanished.

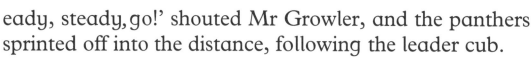

R eady, steady, go!' shouted Mr Growler, and the panthers sprinted off into the distance, following the leader cub.

Today was the school marathon and all the young panthers had to join in. It was also Bobby Blackcat's birthday. But however ill Bobby tried to look, and how-ever much he limped, Mr Growler wouldn't let him off the marathon. Bobby felt very fed up, and shuffled along miserably.

In fact, Bobby felt so sorry for himself, as he mumbled and grumbled about it being the worst birthday ever, that he didn't notice the rather different path that the marathon was taking . . .

It was only when the panthers turned into the front drive of his house that Bobby looked up. There, over the door, was a banner which said, 'Happy Birthday, Bobby!' And underneath the banner stood his parents with a great big chocolate cake.

'Surprise!' shouted the panthers. Even Mr Growler was there, with a large Jungle cocktail in his paw. It was the best birthday ever, and the cubs all agreed that it was *miles* better than being at school.

Clive liked taking photographs. As he lazed on the river-bank close to his home, he would photograph everything he could see.

Click! A picture of a mangrove tree. Click! A photo of dragonflies dancing on the breeze. Click! A picture of the cool blue river as it rolled gently by. Clive would photograph anything.

One day, as he was looking for things to photograph, he saw a small lemur scampering in the branches of a nearby tree.

'I say!' Clive called. 'I'd like to snap you!'

The lemur took one look and ran away as fast as he could. After a short chase, Clive caught up with him. 'All that fuss over a photograph!' cried Clive.

'A photograph!' gasped the lemur, who was puffing and panting. 'I thought you were going to eat me. You are a crocodile, after all.'

'Oh dear, perhaps I shouldn't have said snap!' Clive laughed. Of course, the lemur laughed too, very hard indeed! Clive got his picture, and the two became the best of friends from that moment on.

Sebastian Hippo was taking a morning walk in the jungle. He was just trying to pass between two trees when he realized he was stuck! Sebastian bellowed and roared until his parents found him. They pushed and pulled poor Sebastian with all their might, but he didn't budge. They went to get help.

Hairy-Eared Buffalo pushed from behind. 'Ouch!' cried Sebastian. 'Your horns hurt!'

Red Bush Pig pushed from the front with his flat nose. 'Ouch!' cried Sebastian. 'That hurts!'

Stork flew over and clapped his bill. 'Cover him with mud!' he cried. So they did, but he didn't slide through.

Anhinga Bird, drying her feathers, called, 'Turn him upside down!' They tried.

A passing crane offered his help, but the crowd shouted up, 'Wrong sort of crane!'

Pelican emptied a beakful of water over Sebastian, but it didn't help.

At last, two kindly elephants arrived and quietly pulled the trees apart with their trunks.

Sebastian fell over. 'Thank you!' said the Hippo family, and they all went back to the midday mud.

I love my name,' said Sammy Scaleback. 'You can put so many words with it and it sounds really important.'

'Like what?' asked his mother.

'Well,' said Sammy. 'Like, "I'm Sammy the Snake and I slither and slide smoothly when the sun shines".'

'That's really good,' said his mother.

Sammy went for a walk to see if he could find anyone to play with. Suddenly, he heard a shriek from above, and saw a flash of blue and gold.

'Hello,' said the strange creature.

'Hello,' said Sammy, and drawing in a deep breath he went on, 'I'm Sammy the Snake and I slither and slide smoothly when the sun shines.'

'Well, I'm Paula the Parrot, and I perch in the trees and preen my plumage.'

Sammy was astonished. 'I didn't know anyone else could talk like that!' he said. 'Let's play together and you can be my best friend.'

'Positively perfect,' said Paula.

THE PLAYGROUND

Stevie and Sophie Bushtail lived in a very quiet part of the jungle. There were no cinemas, no fairgrounds, and hardly any young squirrels. One day, as Stevie sat in a tree, dropping nuts on passing buffaloes, he had an idea.

'Let's build an adventure playground!' he said.

His sister thought it was an excellent plan and set to work immediately. Together, they built an obstacle course with mazes, underground tunnels, and hidden doorways. It was a squirrel's dream! When at last they had finished, Sophie said, 'Let's try it!'

They ran up the little ladder, down the tunnel, through the hole in the tree, up the pole, across the river on the swaying bridge, through the maze, and finally ended up in the tree-top house. Of course, it didn't take long before news of the playground spread. Young squirrels from all over the jungle scurried to the famous obstacle course to see if they could do it, and Stevie and Sophie made hundreds of clever new friends.

Henry the sloth yawned and said to himself thoughtfully, 'What shall I do today?'

He searched around for his 'LIST OF THINGS TO DO'. 'Bother,' said Henry, 'I must have left it on Yesterday's tree.' (It was one of Henry's peculiar habits to spend each day hanging from a different tree).

The trouble was that Henry couldn't remember which tree *was* Yesterday's tree. He looked around. The jungle looked very similar in all directions.

Henry had two methods of travelling. Slowly, if he had a definite purpose, or *very* slowly if he wasn't quite sure where he wanted to go. So, moving *very* slowly, Henry began to look about him. He rolled his eyes up and down, left and right, this way and that, until he was quite exhausted. 'It's lost,' Henry sighed. 'I shall have to make a new list.' He wrote carefully the number **1** on a clean sheet of paper. 'Well that's enough for one day. I must look for Tomorrow's tree,' Henry said as he put his pen and paper away.

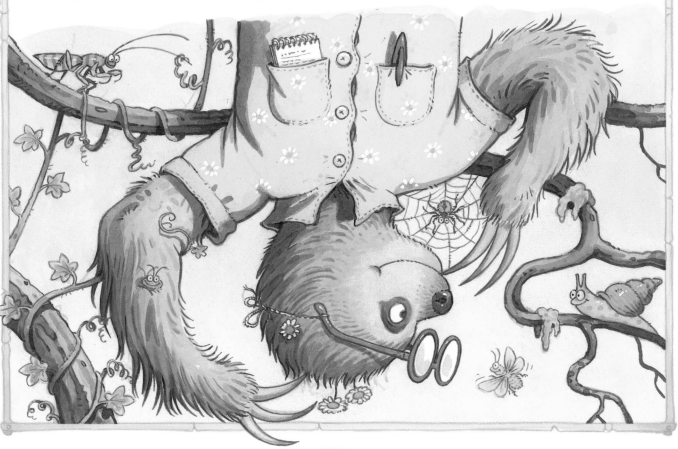

Every frog in the school was jumping about with excitement. The Frog Queen was coming to open the school sports day.

Everyone was wondering who would be this year's champion longjumper. Everyone except for one lonely frog called Fred. Fred knew that whoever won the trophy it wouldn't be *him*. He had never been any good at sports. He was such a poor jumper that he could hardly make it from one lilypad to the next.

At last, the longjump was announced. The eager competitors lined up in front of the Queen. Fred wished he was one of them and sat down feeling sorry for himself. Unfortunately, Fred sat down on a bee! The bee was so angry that it stung him on the backside.

'Yeeooww!' Fred leaped into the air. He sailed over the competitors and the Queen, over the take-off point, over the sandpit, and finally landed yards from the end of the longjump. It was a world record jump. What a hero! All the frogs cheered. They raised Fred on to their shoulders in celebration and the Queen awarded him a big gold medal.

Gina Giraffe was terrified of heights. She had never had the courage to stand up to her full height. Instead, she crawled around on all fours, stretching her neck out in front of her so as to keep her head as close to the ground as possible.

Her mother was worried – Gina was the laughing stock of the jungle. They decided to visit the oldest and wisest giraffe to ask his advice. The wise giraffe said 'Humph' and 'Humm,' and finally, 'Follow me!'

As they got deeper into the jungle, Gina began to smell the most delicious leaves just above her head. She took a bite. The young leaves were sweeter than anything she had ever tasted! Gina began to stretch her neck out to reach the higher leaves. She realized that the higher the leaves grew, the sweeter they tasted. Gina's parents gasped in amazement to see their daughter stretched out to her full height for the first time in her life, munching happily on the topmost leaves. And to this day, Gina has never again been scared of heights.

Percy the Parrot was boasting to his jungle friends. 'Look at me! Look at me!' he cried, in his terrible squeaky voice. 'How beautiful I am. Just look at my wonderful bright colours. You won't see finer plumage anywhere in the jungle.'

Although it was true that Percy was an especially colourful parrot, his friends were bored with hearing it. Night and day, jumping up and down on his perch, Percy would squawk about his fine feathers.

One morning, while Percy was busy preening himself, the other parrots crept up very quietly behind him. Percy was just admiring one blue-green wing as it caught the sunlight, when ALL the parrots let out the most incredibly loud SQUAWK!

It was so loud and unexpected that Percy leapt clean out of his feathers! He had such a fright that he didn't say a word for a week, and when his feathers finally grew back, they were completely white.

Flash was the fastest cheetah in the jungle. He could run from Crocodile Riviera to Monkey Park before you could say, 'Where's Flash?' One moment he was there, then – flash – he was gone.

Flash was also a terrible show-off. 'I'm a hundred times faster than you!' he would boast to Slowcoach the sloth. Despite all his boasting, the animals got together and made Flash a big cream cake for his birthday.

But Flash didn't want to share it, so – flash – he ate it all up and ran into the jungle. It wasn't long before Flash came crawling back to the other animals, looking quite green. 'I feel sick,' he moaned.

'It serves you right for being so greedy and running on a full stomach,' said Slowcoach. 'Come and sit with me for a while and take things easy.'

Flash and Slowcoach played chess all afternoon sitting in a tree, and Flash learned that he didn't have to rush around all the time – he could have just as much fun with his friends. And he never again ate another cream cake all by himself!

Sammy was walking along looking up at the trees. 'What are you doing?' asked Fred.

'It's Christmas tomorrow,' said Sammy, 'and the jungle looks just the same as it does all year round – no snow, no Christmas decorations. It doesn't feel like Christmas at all.'

'Well,' said Fred, 'We could do something about it.'

Fred went home and collected all the Christmas decorations which his family had not used. There were garlands of tinsel, Christmas lights and chocolates in the shape of Father Christmas.

When Sammy saw the pile of decorations that Fred had collected, he asked all the animals for their old decorations, and the whole jungle turned out to help. The giraffes draped the golden tinsel on the highest branches, the elephants threaded the Christmas lights through the forest, the tree frogs carefully hung the baubles, and the monkeys swung about putting chocolates on every branch tip. When they had finished, the whole jungle glittered with red and gold – every tree was a Christmas tree. The animals gazed in awe at the beautiful scene in front of them. On Christmas Day they ate the chocolates and declared that it was the best Christmas ever.

Today was a special day and Mr Edward Elephant was feeling very pleased with himself. He had hired a riverboat to hold a party for his son, Lennie. All their friends were excited about the party too – they chattered, laughed and played non-stop while the boat set off.

'That's odd,' Mr Elephant thought to himself, 'one person is missing. Never mind – I can see Hattie Hippo, playing in the river on her own, so I'll ask her to join us.'

However his invitation was drowned out by a huge *SPLASSSH*. Turning around, Edward could see his son waving at him from the water. Lennie had been chasing the boat on his bicycle but wobbled a little too near the river's edge. 'Oh my,' muttered Edward, 'I've been a forgetful father today and left without my son!'

Fortunately for Lennie, Chris Croc managed to rescue him with his fishing net. After which, everyone partied happily into the night.

It was Kim's first day at school and she felt very shy. Her new school mates crowded around her. 'What kind of animal are you?' they asked.

'I'm a bear,' said Kim.

'We've never seen such a small bear!' hissed Snake. 'You are far too small to be a *grizzly* bear.'

'I'm a koala bear,' said Kim, fearfully.

'And you're too plain to be a *panda* bear,' snuffled Aardvark, who was quite puzzled.

'I told you – I'm a koala bear,' cried Kim, getting quite upset. But no one listened.

'You must be a *teddy* bear,' growled Alligator. At that, the animals all began to shout, 'Teddy bear! Teddy bear!'

Kim made herself as tall as she could and said, 'I may be small but I can climb the tallest trees.'

'Go on then – prove it!' jeered the others.

Kim climbed and climbed until the animals couldn't see her any more. And when she came down again, she brought some delicious honey with her. Kim was the most popular person in the class after that and no one ever mentioned her size again.

Arnold Rhinoceros loved the smell of flowers. When all his friends were out stomping through the jungle and roaring, Arnold would be just as happy gathering a posy of bright forest blooms.

Arnold's parents were worried about him. He was the laughing-stock of the jungle. The parrots made fun of him by perching on his horn, the monkeys pinched his tail and the deer tapped on his thick scaly skin, but Arnold didn't mind. He just carried on sniffing the sweet flowers and humming a pretty tune to himself.

One day, while Arnold was strolling along the river bank, he met Big Ted the tiger. *Everyone* was afraid of Big Ted. The tiger roared ferociously, and bared his huge teeth at Arnold. The animals held their breath, wondering what gentle Arnold would do. But Arnold had just taken an extra big sniff of a jungle flower, and his nose was beginning to tickle . . .

'Aatchooo!' sneezed Arnold. It was the loudest, most terrifying noise Big Ted had ever heard – and he didn't scare easily. He turned on his heels and ran off as fast as he could!

How the other animals laughed – and they *never* teased Arnold again!

ALAN ANT'S ADVENTURE

The ants of Anthill Mountain were busy collecting food. Alan was helping his friends lift a leaf, when, suddenly, the twig he was standing on began to rise up into the sky, taking Alan with it!

Alan peered along the twig and saw a long beak and a large eye at the other end. The twig was in a bird's mouth! Alan (who was afraid of heights) gulped and shut his eyes.

At last, the bird came to a stop at her nest, high up in a tall tree. Alan gazed down at the ground far below. How would he ever get down there and find his way home? Alan was just about to cry, when he heard a chirpy voice.

'Hello! How did you get up here?' It was a flying squirrel. Alan told the squirrel his story.

'Don't worry!' said the friendly squirrel. 'Climb on my tail and I'll get you home. Anthill Mountain is quite near my tree.'

And so the two of them flew back down to earth, where Alan was quite a hero. After all, no ant had ever travelled on both a bird and a squirrel, all in one day!

Wind was roaring through the jungle. Trees swayed and bent their heads. Leaves and branches flew through the air. The birds and animals hid and hoped the storm would soon pass.

Hobart was a very tiny bird. He hung on to the edge of his nest as it rocked to and fro. Suddenly the branch snapped, and, with a terrified wail, Hobart went sailing into the air.

The wind tossed him and twirled him and blew him right to the edge of the jungle. Below him lay the river.

The wind dropped poor Hobart down towards the dark water. He tried to flap his wings and fly back towards the trees, but he wasn't strong enough. He hit the water with a loud splash – and then began to rise right up into the air again! Something warm and firm was under his feet. It was Hippo's back.

Hippo had been hiding from the wind under the water and had chosen just that moment to come out and see what was happening. Just in time to save Hobart.

Sloth was slowly crawling along upside-down under a tree branch, minding his own business when, THUMP! something leapt onto the branch and nearly shook him off. He curled his toes tighter on the shaking branch and looked up. It was Tree-Frog.

'Come on, slowcoach!' said Tree-Frog in his croaky voice. 'You'll never get anywhere going that slow. You'll never win any races! Look at me! I'll be out of sight before you've moved two paces!'

The boastful Tree-Frog hopped away, still laughing to himself. At the end of the branch, he stopped to get ready for the leap to the next tree. 'Watch me, slow-coach!' he shouted and leapt forward. But Tree-Frog had been so busy boasting that he didn't look where he was going and, instead of landing safely on another branch, he crashed into the tree trunk and fell to the ground, stunned.

When Tree-Frog came round, he got to his feet and looked around him. There was Sloth, sitting in the next tree, waiting. 'Sometimes,' said Sloth calmly, 'it pays to go slow.'

Tony, the spotted deer, noticed a tickling feeling in his antlers. He looked up and was amazed to see a little bird perched happily on the top branch of his right antler. Tony couldn't believe his eyes. Not only was the little bird chirping merrily to herself, but she also seemed to be building a nest!

'I get so bored sitting on my eggs with the same scenery to look at day after day,' Henrietta the bird said. 'This year, I can sit on my eggs and you can take me with you to see lots of interesting new sights.'

Tony shouted, raged, pleaded and begged Henrietta to build her nest somewhere else but it was all in vain. She wouldn't move.

Tony carried Henrietta everywhere until her eggs hatched and, at last, it was time for Henrietta and her new chicks to fly away. Strange to say, Tony was very sad to say goodbye! He made Henrietta promise to build her nest in his antlers every year. So if you ever see an antelope with a nest in his right antler, you will know for sure who he is.

Kinkajou's friend was ill and couldn't get out to find food so Kinkajou promised to bring him something to eat. He went into the jungle to gather fruit, which is what kinkajous like to eat.

Wandering through the jungle, he came to a bush covered with luscious berries. He ate some himself. In fact he ate as many as his tummy would hold. Then he started to pick some to take home to his friend. The berries were small and slippery and Kinkajou wondered how he was going to carry them home to his friend without dropping any.

While he was thinking, he heard a rustling behind him. It was Porcupine.

'I have an idea,' said Porcupine. 'Stick the berries on my spines and I'll walk with you to your friend's home and you can unload them there.'

So that is what they did, and a very strange sight Porcupine made walking through the jungle that day!

Let's play hide-and-seek!' Christopher Crocodile said to Stripey the zebra and a little lizard called Lois. 'You both hide and I'll try to find you.'

As it was very warm, Christopher took off his jacket. He put it on a tree-stump, then closed his eyes and counted slowly to ten. Afterwards, he soon spotted Stripey behind a bush.

'It's not fair,' grumbled the zebra. 'I'm easier to find than Lois because I'm so much bigger!'

Christopher could not see Lois anywhere. He asked Stripey to help find her. But as the sun began to sink, there was still no sign of Lois, although they both kept searching and calling.

'Oh! She must be lost,' said Stripey.

'We won't give up looking!' replied Christopher.

It was cooler now. He pulled on his jacket and slipped his hands into its pockets. Suddenly, Christopher gasped in surprise and carefully lifted out Lois from inside one of them.

'Found you!' he cried.

'You took your time,' yawned Lois. 'It was so cosy in there, I fell asleep!'

'You were playing hide-and-sleep!' joked Stripey.

Antony the ant-eater had a problem. He hated eating ants! He quite liked flies and even worms. He loved wild mushrooms and grass with the dew still on it. Now and again he would eat a few black bugs. Sometimes the monkeys would pick bananas for him and peel them with their fast fingers. But ants! Yuck!

He felt a failure. All the animals in the jungle ate what they were supposed to eat. Giraffe browsed slowly through the jungle, eating the leaves from the high branches and Sloth crawled along branches lower down and ate the leaves and fruit that grew there. Owl and Snake ate mice and small creatures and Bear ate honey and fished in the river. He was the ant-eater and he hated ants!

Antony wandered home wondering what he could do. Outside his door he saw Chimpanzee busy with a paint pot. 'There you are,' he said. 'I've solved your problem.' On the door was painted ANTONY THE ANT-HATER. 'I've changed your name!'

George was playing in a clearing, happily kicking around his football, when he accidentally kicked it over a fence into a garden.

George knew that a family of porcupines owned the garden. He had heard terrible tales about them, and he was too scared to ask for his ball back. He was just walking sadly away, when a head popped over the top of the fence, and a beautiful soft voice spoke to him.

'Hello,' said the stranger. 'Is this your football?' She timidly handed the ball to George. 'I'm Penelope Prickles,' she said. 'What's your name?'

'George,' said George. 'Are you really a porcupine? My friend said you would poke me with your spikes if I spoke to you.'

'Oh no,' said Penelope. 'Porcupines only do that if they don't like someone. I thought lion cubs were fierce and would scratch me with their claws and deafen me with their roar. You don't seem like that to me. Come over the fence and we'll play football together.'

And George did just that. Later that afternoon, George and Penelope decided that lion cubs and porcupines could make very good friends after all.

O h no!' cried Billy. 'There's only one banana left. The greedy monkeys have eaten all the rest!'

The last banana was hanging at the very top of a tall banana tree, and Billy was afraid of heights. Every time he tried to climb the long tree, he would feel dizzy, and have to climb down again.

'I'm so hungry,' grumbled Billy. 'I must reach that banana somehow.'

Just then, Jerry the giraffe came by. 'Am I glad to see you!' cried Billy.

'What's wrong, Billy?' asked Jerry, stooping his long neck down so that he could hear Billy's angry squeaks.

'I'm so very hungry, and I can't reach that banana at the top of the tree,' said Billy.

Jerry raised his long neck, took the banana between his teeth and plucked it from the tree. Bending his head down again, he gave it to Billy.

'That's what comes of having friends in high places!' said Billy, proudly.

Silly Sidney was always losing things. Yesterday he had lost his way home. Today he had lost his tail. This is how it happened . . .

Silly, as his friends called him for short, had wrapped himself around the trunk of a small tree. His body was coiled round and round and his head was resting on a short branch that stuck out just below an interesting looking hole.

Silly hoped the hole might be the home of some little animal that would be nice to eat. He kept quite still and watched the hole. Nothing came out.

That was when he noticed that his tail had disappeared! He panicked! He stopped thinking about dinner. He slid his head from the branch and began to unwind himself from the tree.

Round and round he went. Lower and lower, until the last bit of him slithered along the ground. And there was his tail, right at the very end of him! Silly Sidney hadn't lost it, it had just been out of sight at the back of the tree!

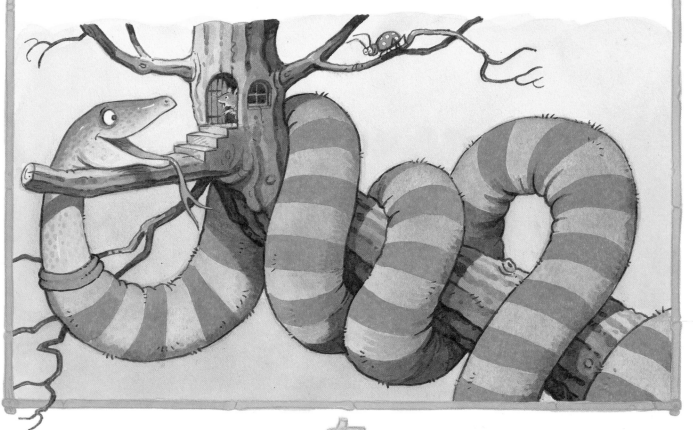

C roak! Croak!' The reeds at the edge of the jungle shivered and shook as Basil Bullfrog practised his baritone.

'Stop that horrible noise!' shouted the dragon-fly that lived near the river. 'I can't stand it any more!'

'But I have to practise,' said Basil. 'It's the concert tomorrow!'

'Well, you'll drive the audience away if *you* sing' snapped the dragon-fly, rudely. Basil sighed.

The next day, all the animals gathered on the riverbank to hear the Frog Chorus. Frogs had hopped for miles to join in the concert. They sat together on the huge lilypads that grew in the river and began to sing. High and loud, soft and low, they croaked and croaked and the animals on the bank swayed in time to the tunes. Suddenly a horrible, rasping 'Croak! Croak!' sounded over the singing.

'Croak! Croak!'

The animals turned to look at Basil – and saw what he had seen. Claud the crocodile was creeping up on the Frog Chorus, ready to eat them. The Frog Chorus fled! Only Basil's loud warning had saved them in time – and frightened away the crocodile!

Tiger strolled through the jungle being tigerish.

First of all, he slipped silently through the long, dried grass that was almost the same colour as his tawny coat and frightened a family of mice having a picnic.

Then he crept behind a tree and leapt out on two monkeys sitting in its shade. They shrieked with fright, jumped to their feet, crashed into each other, and finally ran off, gibbering excitedly.

He pushed his head through a bush and said 'Boo!' to an alligator lying in the shallow water at the river's edge. Alligator had just opened his mouth to have a good yawn but he gulped in a mouthful of river water instead. He was still spluttering as Tiger sneaked away.

Finally, Tiger lay silently on a tree branch that stuck out over the path, until a tortoise and a lizard came by, chattering and laughing. When they were under his tree he jumped onto the ground in front of them. They were so frightened they leapt right into the air.

Tiger went home, laughing. It had been a particularly good day.

CARNIVAL TIME!

I t was carnival time in the jungle. Every year, the wise old lion would choose a new carnival king. Today, hundreds of noisy animals clamoured for his attention, each one desperate to be king for a day . . .

'I'm the best flying acrobat there ever was!' declared Rick, the spider monkey.

'But you need a sedate and dignified king – like me,' said Edgar the sloth.

'You can't change your colour, though! Now *that's* what the crowd wants!' said Jerry the chameleon.

Mick, the shy giraffe, only watched, wondering who would be chosen. But the lion saw him standing silently behind the others and said, 'And what can *you* do?'

The other animals laughed. 'What can *he* do? Why, he's too shy to do anything!' they said.

'We'll see about that,' said the lion, angrily. 'Because he will be this year's carnival king!' At that, the lion smiled kindly at Mick, and said, 'I'm sure there's *something* you can do . . .'

And sure enough, when the king's float came by, the animals could hardly believe their eyes. For there was Mick Giraffe, in a pair of black shades and a spiked mane, but most amazing of all, he was playing the saxophone! The crowd danced and cheered. 'What a talent!' they cried. And Mick smiled proudly. He didn't feel a bit shy.

acaw loved bright things. If he saw anything small and shiny, he would pick it up and take it home to add to his collection.

One day, he was flying home with a bright ribbon he had found floating on the river, when he dropped it. Down and down it fell, right into a deep well. Macaw flew down and peered into the well. The ribbon was floating in the water. 'Oh, bother!' said Macaw, angrily.

Just then, Baboon came along. Macaw explained what had happened and Baboon looked down into the well. 'I can't reach it,' he said. 'But I have an idea.'

Baboon picked up a heavy stone and dropped it down the well. The water rose a little. Baboon kept on dropping stones into the water until the ribbon rose up with the water and he could reach it with his long arms. He fished it out and gave it to Macaw.

'Thank you,' said Macaw, who was very impressed. 'You're nearly as bright as my ribbon!' And he flew happily home with his treasure.

Don't do that!' said Lizzie, crossly. 'Don't change your colour while you're talking!'

'I can't help it,' said Chameleon. 'It's what I do!'

'Well I can't concentrate on what you're saying,' said Lizzie, 'and it was just getting exciting. What is this secret magic you know?'

Chameleon sighed and slowly changed a light brown colour to match the branch he was sitting on. He settled himself more comfortably and went on with his story.

'And so,' he said. 'My great, great grandfather who was called Grey Lizard, learned from a magician the secret of being invisible and from that day on, all his children and all his children's children have been able to make themselves invisible by changing the colour of their skin to match the rocks and branches and leaves they rest on. That's the secret magic!'

'Is that all?' said Lizzie (who was really rather envious of Chameleon's magic), and she slid from the branch and scuttled off home.

'Yes, that's all!' replied Chameleon as he flicked out his long tongue to catch a passing fly.

Every day, after school, Baby Koala's mother would come to collect him. He would cling on to her soft fur while she climbed high into the trees to their home. And every day, Baby Koala would watch Baby Kangaroo climb into his mother's warm pouch, and be taken home in the fastest, most exciting ride imaginable.

'Oh, how I wish I could sit in a pouch and fly through the air in great leaps!' said Baby Koala one day.

'And I wish I could be lifted up high into the tree tops,' sighed Baby Kangaroo, enviously.

'Let's swap!' said Baby Koala. And that is just what they did. When their mothers came to pick them up, it was Baby Kangaroo who held on to Koala's fur, and Baby Koala who sneaked into Kangaroo's pouch.

The trouble was that, half way up the tree, Baby Kangaroo began to feel rather afraid. As for Baby Koala, the more leaps Kangaroo made, the more ill he began to feel . . .

'Don't go any higher!' shouted Baby Kangaroo.

'Oh, please stop jumping!' cried Baby Koala, at last.

And ever since then, Baby Koala is happy to cling to his mother's fur, and Baby Kangaroo is very glad to be safely tucked away in his mother's pouch again!

Lois the ring-tailed lemur was born without a single white ring on her tail. No one knew why, but her tail was just pure black. Lois tried painting the rings on her tail. It worked very well – until she went swimming and the rings washed away. She made some bracelets to put around her tail, but they made it so heavy that she could hardly lift it. So Lois gave up trying. Instead, she decorated her tail with pretty ribbons, but she still wished for the white tail rings of the other lemurs.

One day, Lois was sunbathing in a quiet spot all by herself. She was just dozing off in the warm sun when, suddenly, Jiminy Kangaroo came leaping out of the undergrowth. 'Boo!' he said. Lois nearly jumped out of her skin! At any rate, she jumped clean out of her tail ribbons. Jiminy roared with laughter, and then, quite suddenly, stopped . . .

'Lois!' he said. 'Just *look* at your tail!' And Lois did. There were the stripes, every last one in the purest white.

'I'm a ring-tailed lemur at last!' she cried. And no one ever really knew how Lois got the rings on her tail. I suppose it must have been the shock . . .

Cassie was in a temper, as usual. She crashed through the forest, leaving a trail of broken stalks and leaves behind her. She could hear the animals saying, 'There she goes again – Crosspatch Cassie!'

After a while, Cassie stopped for breath. She didn't mean to be ill-tempered. She wanted to have friends, but she was shy and awkward and that made her cross. Just then, she heard a soft whimper. Peering under a bush, she saw a baby lemur looking at her with its large brown eyes. 'I'm lost!' he said.

Cassie was so surprised she forgot to be shy or bad-tempered. Instead, she bent down and carefully lifted the little lemur onto her back, and set off for his home.

The whole jungle had been searching high and low for him. You can imagine how they cheered when they saw the lost lemur arriving home on Cassie's back. Mrs Lemur hugged her, gratefully. 'Cassie,' she said, 'You're really not a crosspatch after all!'

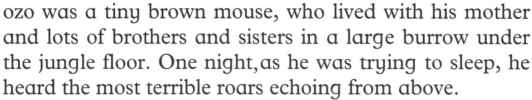

ozo was a tiny brown mouse, who lived with his mother and lots of brothers and sisters in a large burrow under the jungle floor. One night, as he was trying to sleep, he heard the most terrible roars echoing from above.

Zozo crept out of the burrow and, by the light of the moon, made his way towards a dark shape in the clearing. It was Ricky the tiger, and he was rubbing his paw against a tree and groaning.

Zozo scurried up Ricky's leg and on to the huge paw. There, deep in the pad, a sharp thorn was buried. The little mouse seized it firmly in his strong teeth, and pulled, and pulled, and pulled. Pop! Out it came at last, and down Zozo fell.

'Thank you, little mouse,' said Ricky. 'Now, let me take you home.'

Zozo's brothers and sisters had to rub their eyes when they saw their little brother coming home – on the back of Ricky the tiger!

Ben was a little bird, who lived high in the trees on the edge of the jungle. Henry was a big hippo, who lounged lazily in the river. They weren't the sort of animals you'd think would ever meet. Until the day that Ben flew down to drink at the river, and Henry seemed an excellent perching place. Ben began to pick out all the grubs and bugs in Henry's skin. These fed Ben and made Henry very happy. It wasn't at all surprising that the two became the best of friends. If they went walking through the jungle, Ben would fly above Henry, and call out to him if anything dangerous was in the way, or if someone was coming that Henry would rather not meet.

When they went on the river, Ben would sit on Henry's head while he swam slowly along. They did look a strange couple, but when the other animals saw them together, they only smiled and said, 'There go Little and Large'.

Why, Dad, why do we have a curly tail?' asked Little Boar.

'Well,' replied his father, 'it's so that our tails don't drag on the ground and get dirty.'

'Why, Dad, why do we have four feet?' Little Boar went on.

'Well, we need four feet to run fast and get away from our enemies. Now why don't *you* run along and play with your friends,' said Daddy Boar, who was getting tired of all these questions.

But Little Boar wasn't satisfied. 'Why, Dad, why is the jungle called the jungle?' he asked.

'Well, son,' Daddy Boar sighed. 'Because it sounds like tangle, which plants in a jungle get into. Now, will you please leave me in peace.'

'But why, Dad, why are you called a *wild* boar?' persisted Little Boar. 'I mean other animals are just squirrels, parrots or bears.'

'Stop asking me stupid questions or I will chase you and catch you up and eat you for dinner!' cried Daddy Boar in a fury.

Little Boar scampered off as fast as he could go, but at least he had the answer!

Mr Elephant was always in a bad mood when he came home from work. The animals would quake and tremble to hear his steps thudding through the jungle, and scurry away until he had passed. Until, one day, a little mouse got caught in Mr Elephant's path . . .

'Watch out!' he squeaked. 'You'll tread on me!'

Mr Elephant looked down at the miniature creature trembling beneath his huge foot.

'Hmph!' Mr Elephant said. 'What good is such a tiny mouse, anyway?'

'Let me climb up to your ear, and I'll tell you,' said the brave mouse. So he clambered up Mr Elephant's tie, and squeaked in his ear. The animals were astonished to hear Mr Elephant roar with laughter.

'What a good joke!' giggled Mr Elephant, who already felt much better. He carried the little mouse all the way home, and made him promise to tell him a joke every day. Now, the only thing that thunders through the jungle when Mr Elephant comes home from work is his booming laughter!

Nancy was crying. The apes were holding their annual jungle ball tomorrow night. There was a prize for the best dressed, but she would not be going because she had nothing to wear.

The others were clever with their fingers. They could make beautiful dresses out of leaves and reeds, long grasses and vines. Nancy was hopeless. Whatever she made fell apart, or withered before she could wear it.

A touch as light as feathers made her stop crying. On her hand was a beautiful butterfly.

'Why are you sad?' asked the butterfly. Nancy explained.

'Just leave it to me,' said the butterfly. 'You shall be the prettiest at the ball!'

The next night, the apes gathered. They looked around for Nancy, but she was nowhere to be seen. Suddenly, everyone gasped. Into the clearing walked Nancy, in a costume that shimmered and glowed with colour and beauty. No one had ever seen anything like it. For clinging to Nancy were hundreds of butterflies! And that night, Nancy won the prize.

Nina Long-Snake was getting too heavy to dangle from her favourite branches – often they snapped, and she fell to the ground and hurt herself. The doctor put her on a diet and told her to come and see him in three days' time.

She moaned and groaned. She complained that she was hungry all the time, and would surely waste away to nothing if she did not eat something soon. Finally, after three days, Nina slithered off to the doctor's again.

The doctor weighed her. 'You haven't lost any weight,' he said. 'Have you stuck to the diet?'

'Of course!' wailed Nina. 'All I've eaten is one little lettuce leaf!'

The good doctor laughed. 'You are a terrible liar!' he said. 'I can see for myself what you have been eating. Is that the shape of a chocolate bar sticking out? Is that a bag of candy? And what's this lump here? Looks just like a very large slice of cake to me!'

'I never get away with anything,' grumbled Nina, as she slithered home again on a second diet.

The crocodile was dozing by the river in the soft oozy mud, warming his scaly body, when a little bird fluttered down to have a drink in the river.

'Ahem, er, excuse me, but this is such a perfect day, is it not?' smiled the crocodile, trying not to bare his teeth.

'Oh, yes, it is beautiful,' said the bird.

'It would be the most perfect day of my life, if only I didn't have this little stone caught between my teeth. You birds are so lucky not having teeth, you really have no idea of how uncomfortable it is.' He opened his large jaws and said, 'Can you see it?'

'No, I'm afraid not,' said the little bird.

'Come closer and you may be able to pick it out with that clever little beak of yours.' But the little bird was not so foolish. Instead of hopping into those gloomy gaping jaws himself, the bird rolled a stone into the crocodile's mouth. 'SNAP!' went the crocodile's teeth, right onto the stone. 'Aargh!' roared the wicked crocodile.

'How's your toothache now?' laughed the little bird, as he flew away.

Osborne the Parrakeet was the jungle comedian. There was no end to his little jokes, pranks and impressions. He impersonated Sloth running a race, he made jokes about Alligator's false teeth, and told the story of Rhinoceros's unsuccessful diet. The trouble was that, after a while, Osborne's little act wasn't funny anymore. In fact, it made some animals VERY angry indeed!

'Can't you take a joke?' chirped Osborne.

'No!' they growled. The animals decided to give Osborne a taste of his own medicine. When he went to sleep on his perch one night, the monkeys scurried up Osborne's tree, and neatly tied his wings together.

The whole jungle gathered together under Osborne's tree to watch the spectacle! And sure enough, when Osborne woke, he took off from his perch to fly down to the ground and, in midair, he realized he could barely fly at all! Osborne shrieked in horror. Luckily for him, the animals had fixed a net under his perch. Osborne landed gently and bounced up into the air again, chirping furiously.

'Can't you take a joke?' they laughed. And Osborne was very careful who he joked about after that!

ANTON'S FLYING LESSONS

Anton Pterodactyl was a terrible flyer. When his friends saw him flying through the air, wings flapping crazily and feet outstretched, they would scatter as fast as they could before he crash-landed on them.

One day, a famous stunt master came to visit the neighbourhood. It wasn't long before he saw Anton flapping about clumsily in the sky, and landing in a flurry of wings and squawks in the dirt. He laughed and laughed. 'My!' exclaimed the great stunt bird. 'I know why you have such trouble flying—you've got a tiny body, but your wings are enormous!'

'What can I do?' asked Anton, miserably.

'What can you do?' replied the stunt master. 'With my help, you can be the greatest flyer on Earth with wings like that!'

And every day, Anton took flying lessons with the great stunt master, until he could fly with more grace and speed than the grand master himself. His friends were amazed to see the new Anton, swooping, diving, and looping fantastically through the air. Flying was no longer a painful way of getting about to Anton—it was his greatest joy in life.

TOMATOES AND CREAM

Old Lizzie Stegosaurus was especially fond of large red tomatoes. She liked to eat them with cream, just like strawberries. Lizzie grew her tomatoes at the bottom of the garden, and was planning to enter them in the Pre-historic Garden Competition—she was very proud of them and was determined to win first prize.

On the big day, Lizzie carefully gathered and polished the largest and roundest tomatoes. She put them on the judging table, and waited, nervously, for the results. 'The winner,' said the judge, 'of the tomato competition . . . goes to Mr Kritosaurus of Swampville!'

Lizzie was furious. She picked up her tomatoes, and swept out of the room. But then, she had a very naughty idea . . .

Lizzie slipped her tomatoes onto the strawberry table just as the strawberry judging began. 'My!' exclaimed the judge, looking at the basket of tomatoes. 'Those are the biggest strawberries I have EVER seen. I pronounce them the winners of this year's strawberry competition!'

Lizzie was delighted. 'I knew he was extremely short-sighted,' she thought. 'Otherwise, he'd have known that no tomatoes are more beautiful than mine!'

TILLY'S TOYS

Tilly was going to America to stay with her cousins. For at least the fifth time that afternoon she'd packed and repacked her own little suitcase. But she *still* couldn't get her toys to fit in, and she really did want to take all of them to show to her cousins.

Then she had an idea. Very carefully she opened her parents' suitcase, took out the top layer of clothes and replaced them with the rest of her toys. 'They won't need all those clothes anyway!' Tilly thought.

Next morning, in America, Tilly awoke to the sounds of her father's angry roars. There he was, standing in the hallway, wearing nothing but his underwear! 'My clothes have been stolen!' he cried.

'No they haven't,' Tilly confessed.

The truth was told and her father, dressed in Uncle Ron's clothes, didn't seem so cross.

'Well,' he said. 'You'd better go and show your toys to William and Benjamin. It's caused a lot of trouble bringing them here!' He gave Tilly a big wink and then went to try on Uncle Ron's baseball cap.

TERRIBLE TOOTHACHE

Dinosaurs do not clean their teeth every night. In fact, they usually forget to clean them at all.

Harriet *never* cleaned her teeth, and this may have been the reason why she had such terrible toothache. It was so bad that Harriet couldn't sleep. Indeed, she roared with pain so loudly that everyone in the entire house woke up!

Harriet's mother comforted her and Harriet stopped roaring. Harriet's father went back to sleep. Grandma had an idea . . . She tied one end of a very long string to Harriet's tooth, and the other end to the open door. When Grandma shut the door, the string pulled tight and Harriet's tooth popped out! At last, the pain had stopped and everyone could go back to bed.

Of course, Harriet didn't mind losing a tooth because she still had one thousand, nine hundred and ninety-nine others!

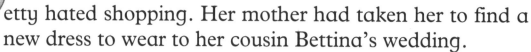

etty hated shopping. Her mother had taken her to find a new dress to wear to her cousin Bettina's wedding.

'I hate dresses,' said Letty. 'Why can't I wear jeans?'

'You can't wear jeans to a wedding, Letty,' said her mother. 'Everyone else will be all dressed up. This is a lovely dress, Letty,' she said, picking one off the rail. 'Why not try it on?'

'I don't like frills,' complained Letty.

'Well how about this one? It's such a nice colour,' said Mrs Lesothosaurus, choosing another.

'I hate pink,' pouted Letty.

'This one is very pretty,' said her mother.

'Yuck! It's got bows,' moaned Letty.

Letty didn't like any of the dresses in that shop . . . or in any other shop. . .

'Letty Lesothosaurus!' said her mother, finally. 'I'm fed up with you. You can go and choose your own dress!' And she sat down on a street bench, exhausted.

Mrs Lesothosaurus was astonished when Letty returned with a dress ten minutes later.

'But it's got *bows*,' she said, 'and *frills* and it's *pink*!'

'Yes, I know,' replied Letty, 'but it's made of denim — just like my jeans.'

Tricky Dicky was a terror. His aunt had given him a big red crayon. Now Tricky Dicky scribbled on *everything*.

'Who's been writing on my new kite?' cried little Horace Hadrosaur (who was very upset).

'Who drew on my nice clean washing?' growled Stan Stegosaur (who did all his own washing).

'Wait 'til I catch the monster who scribbled on my door!' threatened Stan's friend, Lawrence (who always made a lot of noise).

But nobody could catch Tricky Dicky, because he could run even faster than Lightning Larry Lizard (which was very fast indeed).

One day Sneaky Cyril decided to teach Tricky Dicky a lesson.

'I can write my name bigger than you can,' sneered Cyril, writing CYRIL all over a big rock.

'No you can't,' said Tricky Dicky. He pulled out his crayon, hopped on a big stone, and wrote TRICKY DICKY on the biggest rock in the park.

But it wasn't a big rock. It was Terrible Tyrannosaurus Ted, and Tricky Dicky was very careful where he scribbled after that!

It was Easter time, and all the dinosaurs in the neighbourhood were having an Easter egg hunt. They had found ninety-nine of the eggs that Billy had hidden. There was just one more chocolate egg to find. They searched *everywhere*.

'Am I getting closer?' asked Pedro Pentaceratops.

'Oh, you're *very* close,' replied Billy. 'The trouble is, of course, that this egg tends to move about a bit.'

The dinosaurs were very puzzled. They looked under bushes and turned over stones. Ali even disturbed Mrs Allosaurus' nest, and for a moment thought she'd found the egg she was looking for. 'Not those!' cried Mrs Allosaurus.

Finally, the dinosaurs said, 'We give up. Tell us where it is!' Billy smiled. He went over to Pedro Pentaceratops, and pulled out the last chocolate egg from behind his bony neck frill.

'It's been just behind your nose all this time!' And he gobbled it up as quickly as he could, because the egg-hunters looked *very* annoyed!

Jasper Centrosaurus was the boxing champion of Fossil High School for Horned Dinosaurs. No-one had ever managed to beat him, and so Jasper became very conceited, and sometimes, a bit of a bully.

One day, a new dinosaur came to the school. Her name was Meg Tiny Dino because she was very small. When Jasper began to bully her, Meg challenged him to a boxing match. 'But I couldn't possibly fight with *you*!' Jasper laughed. 'It would be far too easy to win.' The dinosaurs tried to persuade Meg not to fight Jasper, but she was determined to teach him a lesson.

All the dinosaurs crowded into the playground to watch the boxing match. Jasper pulled the first punch, but before he could hit little Meg, she had dived straight for his ribs — Meg didn't punch Jasper, she tickled him!

'Hee hee hee,' giggled Jasper. 'Oh no, oh ha ha, stop! Please stop! I give up. You're the champion!'

Meg smiled, and all the dinosaurs cheered. 'I knew you weren't as tough as you look', said Meg. 'Promise never to bully anyone again, or I'll tickle you!' she threatened. And Jasper did — very quickly!

Simon Saurus had been invited to a fancy dress party.

'I'd like to be a fierce monster,' he decided. So Mum made some cardboard claws to fit over his hands and painted a fierce mask. Simon was not impressed.

'How will I eat my tea?' he cried. 'That's no good at all. I want to be a king instead.'

Fortunately, the spiky claws looked like a crown when they were turned upside down, and a bedspread made a splendid cloak. Simon was still not impressed.

'How will I play running-about games with that cloak?' he complained. 'I want to be an explorer.'

Mum stuck the crown on the end of a stick for a spear. They found a backpack and a battered old hat. But Simon was not impressed.

'How will I play Pass the Parcel if I have to hold these?' he grumbled. 'I want to be a . . .'

'No more!' said Mum. 'You can make your own costume!'

When it was time to go, Simon appeared wearing the backpack on his chest, the long cloak, the monster mask on his tail, and the cardboard crown on his head.

'I'm a Sorry-osaurus,' said Simon.

'Well, that's an excellent choice,' laughed his Mum, and they were friends again.

It was Humbert's first day on the ski slopes, and he stood at the top of the mountain, looking down. It looked awfully steep. Just as he was wondering how on earth he was going to pluck up the courage to ski down, he felt himself slipping . . . and before he could stop himself, Humbert was off down the mountainside, picking up speed as he went!'

As he hurtled off, he heard someone shout, 'Oh my goodness, he's heading for the ski-jump!' And sure enough, he was . . .

'Aaargh!' roared Humbert, as he saw the ski-jump ahead of him. Since he didn't have the faintest idea of how to stop himself, Humbert went sailing over the ski-jump, shot into the air, turned head over heels, and landed with a thump at the bottom.

It took quite a while before Humbert's ski-instructor reached the spot where Humbert was lying in a heap, with a bruised tail and a broken spike. 'The first thing I'm going to teach you, Humbert,' he said, 'is how to stop!' But Humbert thought he'd had enough skiing for one day . . .

A SPECIAL PAIR OF SHOES

Alice Scelidosaurus was going to a party, and she wanted a new pair of shoes to wear. 'Come along, Sylvester!' she said to her younger brother, who was busily painting a picture. 'I'll need your advice on which pair of shoes to buy.' The trouble was, Alice had VERY BIG feet. They went from shop to shop, but she couldn't find a single pair of shoes that were large enough.

Alice began to get rather annoyed. 'All dinosaurs have big feet!' she complained. 'Surely there must be *something* large enough for me? After all, I can't go barefoot to the party.'

'I'm afraid your feet are even bigger than most,' said Sylvester, who wanted to go home and finish his picture. 'But I think I may have an idea . . .'

Alice *did* go barefoot to the party, but nobody knew, because Sylvester had painted a fabulous pair of shoes on Alice's feet. 'Oh, Alice!' her friends gasped. 'Where *did* you get your shoes?'

'Oh, I had them made specially for me,' she said, and smiled sweetly.

Roland Styracosaurus was sitting in his maths class, day-dreaming as usual. He was thinking about what he would do if he won the lottery. Would he build a swamp adventure playground all for himself? Or would he buy a chocolate factory? Perhaps he would travel the world in a private aeroplane . . .

'Roland!' shouted Mr Megalosaurus, crossly. 'I'm talking to you!'

Roland looked up in fright at the blackboard on which Mr Megalosaurus had written a very long sum. 'Oh no!' he thought to himself. 'He must want me to answer that horrible-looking sum.' Roland made a wild guess. 'Fifty-four,' he said.

'No!' replied Mr Megalosaurus.

'Five hundred and two,' said Roland, hopefully.

'NO!' said Mr Megalosaurus, in a voice that made Roland quake.

'Three hundred and eight?' said Roland, in a very small voice.

Mr Megalosaurus sighed. 'I said it's time to go home, you *silly* dinosaur!'

Roland looked about him, and saw that the class room was deserted. 'Oh, thank you, Mr Megalosaurus!' he said, and hurried off home!

The dinosaurs were having a picnic in the park. The sun was shining and there was lots to eat. When everyone had eaten their fill, and the adults lay down sleepily in the sun, Barry said, 'Let's play on the slide!'

The children ran off towards the slide, but when Daisy set eyes on it, she began to cry.

'Whatever's the matter, Daisy?' burped Big Morton Megalosaurus when he saw her tears.

'Someone has broken the slide. I was having such a lovely day, and now it's spoiled.'

'Cheer up Daisy,' grinned Morton. 'I've got an idea. Come over here and stand on my tail.'

Puzzled, Daisy stepped on to Big Morton's tail. He suddenly ducked his head down, lifted his tail in the air, and Daisy slid all the way down his back! Daisy and Barry took turns on Morton's sliding tail all day long, and thought it was much more fun than the slide.

'Oh, Morton, that was great fun,' said Daisy. 'You've saved the day!'

Neville Saltasaurus just loved taking baths. He liked to have bubbles spilling over the side of the tub, and animal-shaped soaps, and extraordinary bath toys. He could lie in the bath for hours. The only trouble was that Neville was really too big for the bath—he always had to dangle his tail over the edge where it would soon get cold.

One day, Neville was lying in the bath as usual, thinking hard about how he could manage to keep his tail warm and make his bathtimes really perfect. Suddenly, he heard his sister Mandy, shouting.

'Oh no!' she cried. 'I'll never be able to knit! Look at this jumper—it's such an odd shape, and it's far too big!'

Neville had just had an idea . . . Leaping out of the bath with a great splash, he thundered downstairs, leaving wet footprints everywhere. 'I'll have it!' he panted. Neville slipped the jumper over his tail. It was a perfect fit. Mandy smiled. Neville need never have a cold tail in the bath again!

Billy Brontosaurus loved to play football. But the other dinosaurs wouldn't let him play in their game.

'You are much too clumsy,' groaned Freddy, whom Billy had knocked over with his tail.

'Your big feet make huge craters in the pitch,' squeaked Dilly, scrambling out of an *enormous* footprint.

'Popwhoossh,' hissed the ball when Billy accidentally trod on it.

'You can't play with us,' they all said. 'Go away!'

Billy nearly cried. He could only watch as the other dinosaurs played his favourite game. They scored lots of goals and were having a great time. Then, Freddy kicked the ball so hard it flew into a tree. Nobody could reach it. They jumped up and down and threw sticks at it, but still the ball was stuck.

Suddenly, with a plop and a bounce, the ball rolled on to the pitch again! Billy had stood on his back legs, reached up with his long neck, and plucked the football from the tree!

'Hurrah for Billy!' shouted Dilly.

'You can play football with us any time,' said Freddy.

Billy was very happy.

I wish we had a garden,' sighed Jemima as she gazed out of the window. It was a hot day and she could see her friend Daniel Diplodocus pruning his roses next door, but Jemima's family didn't have a garden. They lived in a first floor flat.

'We could make a garden,' said her dad.

'Could we really?' asked Jemima excitedly.

'Yes,' said her dad. 'I'll show you how.'

So that afternoon Jemima and her dad bought some seeds (Dad said cress were best for a small garden). They filled an old tin foil cooking tray with soil and planted the seeds carefully. Then Jemima watered them. She wanted it to look like a real garden, so she arranged pebbles in a line to make a path and cut out a shiny circle of tin foil to make a pond.

Jemima put her garden on a sunny windowsill and watered it every day. By the end of two weeks, it was full of green sprigs as big as her little finger.

'Now comes the best bit,' said Jemima's dad.

'What's that?' asked Jemima.

'We harvest them,' he replied, 'and then we eat them!'

They ate Jemima's cress with buttery toast and boiled eggs. It was delicious.

Cedric was desperate to join the circus. He had been practising all his circus acts for weeks. On the day of the audition, Cedric was very nervous as he met the Circus Manager, but he bravely went into the ring and climbed the long ladder to the trapeze. It was no good. Cedric was just too scared of heights to make the jump.

Next, he showed the Manager his acrobatics. Poor Cedric! He couldn't even do a handstand. The Circus Manager sighed. 'Why not try juggling?' he asked

Cedric *did* try, but he was hopeless! The balls went rolling all over the floor. By this time, quite a crowd had collected to watch the spectacle. They thought it was one of the funniest sights they'd seen in a long time. When the Circus Manager heard the laughter, he suddenly had an idea . . .

'You will be a clown!' he cried.

And Cedric made one of the best circus clowns ever!

Brenda was watching Mummy clear out her wardrobe. All the old clothes went in a pile to throw away and this pile was getting bigger and bigger. Then Mummy found a red dress with bright yellow flowers. It used to be her favourite dress. Mummy tried to put it on but it was far too small. She couldn't bear to throw it away, so she wondered what she could do with it.

'I know!' said Mummy, excitedly. 'I'll use the material to make you a lovely new dress.'

'Yuk!' said Brenda. 'I don't want it,' and she ran into her room to play with her toys.

Later that afternoon, Mummy came into Brenda's room. 'I know who'll appreciate my lovely dress now,' said Mummy, smiling. And she held up two tiny little dresses which she had made that afternoon, that were just right for Brenda's favourite doll and teddy.

Joey loved climbing. He could climb any tree, wall, or fence that he came across, no trouble at all.

One day, his brother Jasper went out to play football with his friends. Joey wanted to go too, but Jasper told him he was too young to play with his friends, and no good at football.

Joey secretly followed his brother to the football field, and hid behind a tree.

A few minutes after the game had started, Michael kicked the football over a garden wall. 'What do we do now?' asked Jasper angrily. 'We'll never get it back!'

'We could fly my new kite,' said Bob. But again, within a few minutes the kite flew up into the air and got stuck in the branches of a tree.

'Oh no!' cried Jasper. 'Now what are we going to do?'

Just then, Joey appeared from behind the tree. 'I'll get them for you!'

Before the boys could answer, Joey was scaling the wall into the garden. A few seconds later, the football flew over the wall back into the field. Then Joey climbed up the tall tree and untangled the kite from the branches with one hand.

When he touched ground again safely, the boys cheered. 'Looks like we'll have to take my kid brother with us every time we go out to play,' smiled Jasper.

Christa was very excited about her birthday party as it was just a week away.

'What shall I wear?' she asked her mother, combing through her wardrobe.

'You can wear this lovely white dress,' said Mummy, 'with your red ribbon.'

But the dress had a dirty smudge on it, so Christa's mummy put the dress in the washing machine and went to find some washing powder.

'She's forgotten my ribbon,' thought Christa and put it into the machine with the dress.

Later that day when Mummy took out the dress it had turned bright PINK!

'My dress!' sobbed Christa. 'I can't wear it and I don't want a party!' she cried.

'Don't worry,' said Mummy comfortingly. 'We can make it into a pink party!'

And all the invitations to Christa's party said, 'Come to my pink party. Everyone must wear something pink!'

Daisy was very good at dancing. When she had learned every dance there was to know, she decided to think up her own.

She practised all afternoon in the living room, moving to the pop music on her stereo. At last, Daisy's new dance was nearly ready.

'I just can't think of an exciting way to finish it,' she said. 'Perhaps my brother will have some ideas.'

She opened Brad's bedroom door and stepped straight onto a marble. She skidded across the floor, hit the bed-post, and did a perfect somersault onto the bed.

'Are you all right, Daisy?' asked Brad. 'That was quite a fall!'

'It wasn't a fall,' said Daisy. 'It was the perfect finale to my new dance!'

ncle Brontosaurus was a very big dinosaur. He was so big that he couldn't fit into any of his clothes. His doctor told him to go on a diet because he was too fat.

Mummy made a special meal for all the family to help Uncle Brontosaurus get thin again. Rachel and Mark thought it was a horrid meal—just a few lettuce leaves and grapes.

'Have you had enough to eat?' asked Mummy.

'Yes, thank you,' said Uncle Brontosaurus. 'That was plenty for me.'

After everyone had gone to bed, Mark began to get rather hungry . . .

He crept downstairs and into the kitchen. He found some cheese, and some slices of ham, and he made himself a very large sandwich. He was just about to take a bite, when he heard footsteps.

'A burglar!' he thought, and dived under the table. He could see the burglar's feet coming nearer, and finally, sitting down at the table!

'I'll get Daddy,' he thought. As he crept out, he saw that the 'burglar' was none other than Uncle Brontosaurus, and he was eating Mark's sandwich!

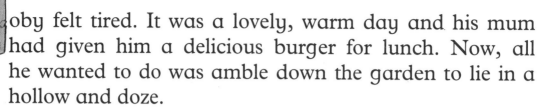

Toby felt tired. It was a lovely, warm day and his mum had given him a delicious burger for lunch. Now, all he wanted to do was amble down the garden to lie in a hollow and doze.

Meanwhile, a few streets away, Toby's friend, Brett, was busy in the front garden. He was helping his dad who had taken down an old fence and was wondering what to put up in its place.

'Shall we have a new ranch-fence or a hedge?' asked dad. 'I can't make up my mind!'

Neither could Brett. 'I'll go and ask Toby what he thinks,' he said.

When Brett arrived at Toby's house, Toby's mum told him that Toby was fast asleep in the hollow at the bottom of the garden. All Brett could see of Toby was the row of big, bony plates that grew along his back.

'I know what dad should build,' grinned Brett, hurrying home, 'a craggy *stone wall*! Toby gave me the idea without even waking!'

Rex woke up with a start. It was very dark outside.

'Terry' he cried, 'wake up!' Terry didn't stir. He was fast asleep.

'Wake up Terry, please!' said Rex. 'There's a giant dinosaur in the garden and I'm frightened.'

Suddenly there was a bright flash of light and Terry sat up in bed with a start. 'It's spitting fire!' he said.

They ran into their parents' room.

'Daddy, Daddy!' said Terry. 'There's a giant dinosaur in our garden, bigger than Uncle Brontosaurus and he's breathing fire and roaring!'

'Come with me,' said Daddy.

He took Terry and Rex by the hand and led them to the window. Just then, the giant spat so much fire that it lit up the whole sky.

'That is lightning,' said Daddy.

Then the giant roared so loudly that it made even Daddy jump.

'That is thunder,' said Daddy.

Then it started to rain.

'It's not a monster,' said Daddy. 'Just a storm. You can go back to bed now.' And Terry and Rex slept soundly all night.

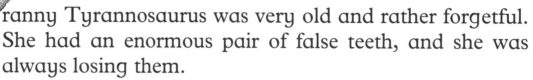

Granny Tyrannosaurus was very old and rather forgetful. She had an enormous pair of false teeth, and she was always losing them.

One day, as usual, Granny Tyrannosaurus said, 'I've lost my teeth.'

Everyone sighed. 'They should be easy to find,' said Mummy — for they usually turned up somewhere.

The family began to search for Granny's teeth. Mummy looked in the kitchen in all the pots and pans; Frances looked in the pond, turning over the water-lilies; Aunt Rose looked in the sitting-room, checking under each cushion; Daddy simply looked everywhere he thought nobody else had looked; but nobody could find the teeth.

'Let's look again after tea,' said Mummy. 'You must all be very tired.'

'Yummy,' said everyone at once, running into the kitchen. The search had made them very hungry.

Frances looked up with a mouthful of cake. 'Oh Gran!' she said.

'Oh Gran!' said Aunt Rose.

'Oh Gran!' said Mummy. 'You are silly. Your teeth are in your mouth!'

Daredevil Dinosaur worked at a film studio. He was specially trained to do stunt flying in all sorts of aeroplanes.

He appeared in lots of action-packed films and everyone called him Daredevil Dinosaur, although that wasn't his real name, of course.

One day, he visited his nephew, Neil, who loved to hear about his uncle's spectacular stunts.

'I'm sure there isn't a plane that you can't fly!' said Neil proudly.

'Not so far,' replied Daredevil Dinosaur.

Then Neil showed him his model aircraft.

'I saved up and bought this,' he said proudly.

Daredevil Dinosaur went to the park with Neil to try it out. Neil made the plane dip and twist in the air, then loop-the-loop.

When Daredevil Dinosaur had a go, it suddenly dived straight for him. Startled, he jumped out of the way just in time before the model crash-landed on the grass.

'Phew!' grinned Daredevil Dinosaur. 'That's the first plane I *couldn't* fly!'

'**M**um, why have I such a long neck?' asked Neville.

'Some dinosaurs just do!' she smiled. 'It can be very useful for looking into tall cupboards or peeping over folk's heads in a crowd,' she went on. 'You're lucky to have a long neck!'

'Am I?' sighed Neville who was not at all sure about that, especially as he had nearly hit his head on the branch of a tree while walking home from school.

Neville's mum had an idea. Next day, she took Neville and his friend, Neil, to visit a maze.

'You two go in and enjoy yourselves,' she said. 'I'll sit here and rest!'

Neville and Neil followed some other visitors as they zig-zagged to the middle of the maze. But no one knew the way out again. They were surrounded by tall hedges.

'What shall we do?' asked Neil.

'Follow me!' grinned Neville. He set off, turning this way and that, and soon arrived at the exit. Everyone cheered, including Neil.

'You're right, Mum!' called Neville happily.

'Long necks are useful for getting out of trouble, too!'

Mine!' shouted Rosie.

'Mine!' shouted Rex.

The terrible Tyrannosaurus twins were arguing over their toy truck. Rosie pulled it one way. Rex pulled it the other. The toy truck was about to break. . .

'If you don't let go,' said Rex, 'I'll dribble all over your dolls' house!'

'And if you don't let go,' said Rosie, 'I'll trample on your favourite teddy!'

'If you don't let go,' shouted Rex, 'I'll break your bike!'

'And if you don't let go,' bellowed Rosie, 'I'll kick your kite!'

'Well if you don't let go,' screamed Rex, 'I'll bash up your bedroom!'

'If you don't let go,' shrieked Rosie, 'I'll stamp on your soldiers!'

'Well, if you two don't stop shouting,' said Mrs Tyrannosaurus, 'there won't be any jelly for tea.'

And you couldn't hear a squeak out of either of them.

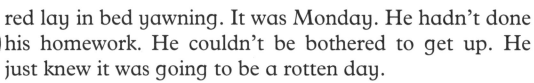

Fred lay in bed yawning. It was Monday. He hadn't done his homework. He couldn't be bothered to get up. He just knew it was going to be a rotten day.

'I don't want to go to school,' his muffled voice told his mum from under the bedclothes.

'Oh, you are so forgetful,' she smiled.

His sisters peered round the door.

'You can't have forgotten,' they giggled.

Fred could hear his father's deep, booming voice chuckling, 'Fred forgetting his head again?'

Well, what if he did sometimes forget things. It wasn't fair to tease him. It was going to be a *very* rotten day. He rolled crossly out of bed, washed and cleaned his teeth as slowly as he could, and then slouched grumpily into the kitchen for breakfast.

But what he found there soon changed his wrinkled frown to a huge grin.

'Happy Birthday, Fred!' cried his family, crowding round with cards, presents and kisses, and pointing to a splendid cake on the table.

'Oh, Fred,' said his mum, 'You are so forgetful!'

Melissa had always wanted a garden of her own. She never forgot to water the seeds in her parents' garden, and was always first to spot the tiny, pale leaves pushing through the soil.

Today spring was in the air, and to Melissa's delight, when she asked if she could plant the seeds today, Mum said, 'Yes, we'll plant them on the left of the path.'

Melissa brought out the trowel and packet of seeds that Uncle Dip had given her for her birthday.

She dug the soil and pulled out the weeds—just as she had seen her mum do. Then she sieved the soil through the garden sieve until it was crumbly—just as she had seen her dad do. She made channels across the earth and sprinkled in her seeds, gently covering them over with her fingers. She watered the seeds and stuck a little marker in the earth with 'Melissa's flowers' written on it. Just as she stood back to admire her work, Mum came into the garden.

Melissa pointed proudly at her handiwork. 'Well,' Mum gasped. 'You are such a good gardener, you had better plant the other side of the path, too!'

And that spring, Melissa's flowers were the most beautiful in the whole garden.

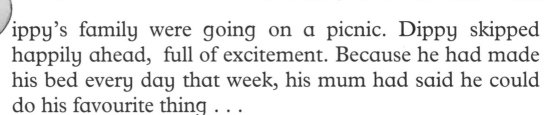

Dippy's family were going on a picnic. Dippy skipped happily ahead, full of excitement. Because he had made his bed every day that week, his mum had said he could do his favourite thing . . .

As he rounded the bend, his twinkling green eyes saw the meadow and the pond, and beyond that, the brown, muddy swamp. With a yell of delight, he bounded off.

His family soon arrived. Mum and Dad settled down on the grass while the little ones played.

Suddenly, a mysterious glugging noise made them turn to the swamp. Great bubbles of mud were growing and bursting on the surface. Then a dome of mud rose from the murky swamp, and two twinkling green eyes blinked wickedly at them. They were frozen to the spot as they watched the shape grow. It was horrible! And it was coming towards them!

'Help! A monster!' the little ones shouted, as the large, brown, dripping beast advanced with a fearful roar.

Then the monster wiped its great paws across its face, smearing the mud from its green eyes and revealing the face of—Dippy!

'It's worth making my bed every day,' he giggled, 'if it means I can jump in the swamp!'

Mark couldn't sleep at night because he was so worried about not making friends at his new nursery.

When he arrived at the nursery, his mother gave him his lunchbox. 'I don't want to go,' he said, but his mother just smiled.

'You'll be all right,' she told him.

Mark wandered in and met the other little dinosaurs. They all looked much more confident than he was. He drew pictures, listened to stories and sang songs with his class, but he still felt too shy to talk to anyone. When lunchtime came, Mark opened his lunchbox. His mother had baked him some ginger cookies. She must have forgotten that Mark hated ginger more than anything else. The day was getting worse . . .

Just then, a pretty little green-skinned dinosaur came up to him and said, 'I'll give you my orange if you give me a cookie . . .'

Mark smiled and said, 'OK!'

Soon, all the children were crowding around him, asking him for cookies. By the end of the day, he'd made friends with everyone in the class.

When Mark got home, he said, 'Mum, can you bake some more ginger cookies? We all loved them!'

Alfred loved singing! He sang in the shower, in bed, on the bus, and especially in other people's houses. He thought his voice was beautiful, and even recorded some of his best songs on his tape deck. But everyone else thought he sounded awful.

'Stop screeching!' yelled his next door neighbour. The postman dreaded delivering his mail, and his other neighbour permanently wore earplugs. But Alfred kept on singing!

Then a new family moved in down the road. They loved Alfred's singing. They asked him over for lots of parties, and always wanted him to sing afterwards. They even borrowed his tape! Alfred felt much happier now that he had friends who liked his voice. With their encouragement he sang even more loudly and more often. Alfred thought his new friends were fantastic. But no-one else did! I wonder why?

Dolly was learning to swim. She was jealous of her brother Darren when he plunged into the rippling water of the pond. And rather cross with him when he leapt up and splashed her with cold spray.

'Go away,' she cried. 'I can swim if I need to.'

'Not without your feet touching the bottom,' he retorted, which was, in fact, almost true. No matter how hard she tried, Dolly could do only two or three strokes before her feet sank to the bottom.

'Today, I will swim,' she said to herself in her most determined way, and splashed off for two and a half strokes before her feet sank again.

Just then, a strong gust of wind blew across the pond. It lifted their clothes and towels on the bank—and blew Dolly's treasured cuddly dinosaur into the water!

'Toothy!' she cried, setting off at once across the water to rescue her beloved friend. Darren could not believe his eyes! Dolly was swimming—really swimming—without a single toe touching the bottom, all the way to Toothy, floating on the pond.

'Bravo!' he shouted as Dolly reached the sopping wet Toothy and dragged him to safety.

'I said I could swim if I needed to!' she said.

Mummy dreaded taking Robbie to the supermarket because he never behaved himself. As she pushed him round the aisles in a trolley, he would knock things off the shelves, leaving a trail of frozen peas or grapes behind them. When Mummy wasn't looking, he would throw chocolates and cookies into the trolley.

'What can I do with him?' Mummy thought in desperation. Then she noticed a little girl sitting quietly in a trolley colouring some pictures in a colouring book.

Next time Mummy went shopping with Robbie she brought along some crayons and a colouring book. Robbie sat patiently colouring in the pictures of dinosaurs, and by the time he'd finished, they were home again.

Mum!' shouted Stephen, rushing home from school. 'I'm in a play and I'm a king and I've got lines to say and a costume and you and Dad must come and it's for Christmas and I must learn my words and . . .'

'Goodness me, do take a breath,' laughed Mum. Stephen couldn't wait to practise.

'Okay,' said Mum. 'I'll say Peter's line first . . . 'Who is this coming to visit the baby king?'

'I am Balthasar and er . . . and . . .' said Stephen, forgetting the rest of the line.

'Beautifully spoken, dear,' said his mum, 'and the words were almost right. Let's try once more.'

'I am Balthasar and I bring um . . . er . . .'

'We'll just keep practising, shall we?' said his mum patiently. And that is what they did.

As the parents waited for the play to begin, none was more anxious than Stephen's mum, for however hard he tried, he could not remember his words. As the kings strode on to the stage, she held her breath.

'Who is this coming to visit the baby king?' said Peter. Stephen stepped forward.

'I am Balthasar and I bring gold for the baby king,' said Stephen. And his mum felt *very* proud.

Oliver Nodosaurus looked extremely fierce and had an enormously loud roar. Mrs Protoceratops, the drama teacher, thought he would be perfect as the big bad monster in the school play.

Although Oliver did *look* very fierce, he was really very shy. He didn't want to be on stage one little bit, but he didn't dare refuse.

On the night of the school play, Oliver had terrible stage fright. He was too scared to go on stage and just stayed behind the curtains.

Just then, little Billy, who was sitting in the audience, saw Oliver's shadow fall across the stage floor. 'Ooh look!' he shouted. 'There's the monster! You can see his enormous shadow!'

The audience thought it was a very clever way to show the monster. It was much more frightening to see just the shadow, and imagine what the monster looked like, than to see an actor playing the part.

'The drama teacher must be *very* clever,' they said. And nobody knew what had *really* happened except Oliver and Mrs Protoceratops, who didn't mind a bit!

Bill and Betty stared through the window at the grey sky.

'We won't be able to go to the park today,' Bill complained. 'Look, it's starting to rain already. And I so wanted to play outside with my friends.'

'Never mind, dear,' said his dad. 'You can play with your toys today, and perhaps it will be sunny tomorrow.'

But they quickly tired of any games. They started to play with first one thing, then another, but they were always drawn back to the window, where the rain streamed down faster and faster by the minute.

'Look at those raindrops,' said Betty gloomily. 'The harder it rains, the faster they go . . . That's it! We can play races with the raindrops.'

In minutes they were utterly absorbed, squeaking and roaring with excitement as first one raindrop, then another cascaded down the window and dashed across the finishing line!

And who won all the races at the end of the day? The dinosaurs were enjoying themselves so much, they quite forgot to count!

Dickon loved playing among the plants at the end of his garden. When he was on his own, he liked nothing better than tracking mini-beasts. Crouching down with his nose pressed to the ground, he would follow the tiny creatures, tracking their every move.

One day, he spotted a big caterpillar. Dickon had never seen such a wonderful creature and he watched, fascinated, as it devoured chunks out of a leaf.

For days Dickon tracked his caterpillar. He had only to follow the trail of nibbled leaves and he was sure to find it. Until one day there was nothing—nothing except a fat brown lump of a thing hanging from a stem. Dickon shuffled off to find his friends. Mini-beast tracking did not seem the same any more.

Some time later, Dickon again came across the fat brown lump of a thing. He gently touched it with his nose. It made a papery, cracking sound, then it slowly split and a slender creature appeared. The crumpled paper on its back stretched out, and before Dickon's astonished eyes, there was a beautiful butterfly. It lifted into the air, circled once as if to say goodbye, then flew away. Dickon's caterpillar had become a butterfly.

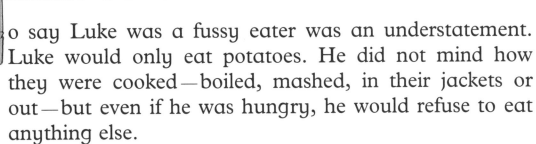

To say Luke was a fussy eater was an understatement. Luke would only eat potatoes. He did not mind how they were cooked—boiled, mashed, in their jackets or out—but even if he was hungry, he would refuse to eat anything else.

'I'm sure there are more things you like than just potatoes!' his mum complained.

Mum was planning the games for Luke's birthday party. Luke loved playing games, especially the surprise games his mum always invented. This year, she planned to surprise him more than usual.

'This game is 'Test your Taste',' she announced to the excited children. 'Put on your blindfolds, then taste the food in bowls and see if you can guess what it is.'

The little dinosaurs poked around with their spoons, managing to smear almost as much food on each other's faces as they got into their mouths! Finally the food-spattered papers were handed in. For every single one, Luke had written, 'Potatoes'!

'I liked them all,' he explained with a grin, 'so I thought they must all be potatoes.'

'But not one of them was potatoes,' laughed Mum, 'so tomorrow you can have something else for tea!'

Monty's sunglasses wouldn't stay on his nose. He bought a red round pair, then a blue star-shaped pair and an orange triangle pair, but they all kept slipping off.

'I have to wear sunglasses or the sun hurts my eyes,' Monty complained, but he couldn't find a pair to fit.

When Monty went to the seaside with his friends he had to sit in the shade as it was a very sunny day.

'Come and play on the beach,' called his friends, but Monty stayed under a tree. Then his best friend Oliver came back from the shops with some ice-cream and a special present for Monty . . .

'Try this on,' he said, and gave Monty a bright red baseball cap. It fitted perfectly, shading his eyes from the sun. Monty was delighted and ran to join his friends playing football on the beach.

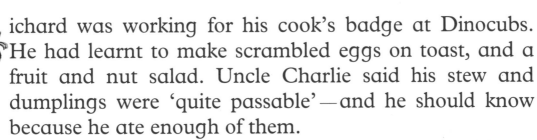

Richard was working for his cook's badge at Dinocubs. He had learnt to make scrambled eggs on toast, and a fruit and nut salad. Uncle Charlie said his stew and dumplings were 'quite passable'—and he should know because he ate enough of them.

But what Richard liked making best were rock cakes—crunchy outside and soft inside, with juicy sultanas in each mouthful. Richard had to bake the cakes at the next Dinocubs meeting. He weighed out the ingredients, but Mum could not find any large enough pots.

'I know,' said Mum, 'just make half the recipe.'

Richard set off, confident that his cook's badge was as good as won. With the flair of an expert chef, he tossed in flour and butter, fruit and egg. The mixture did seem sloppier than usual, but never mind.

Ping! Time to get them out. But what a shock! Instead of crunchy rock cakes, all he could see were soft and rounded pale mud cakes. Richard hung his head. What about his badge now? Dinoleader said nothing. When they were cool, he took a bite.

'These mud cakes are as tasty as your rock cakes,' he said. 'You have earned your badge.' He realized what Richard and his Mum had not. When they halved the recipe, they forgot to add only half the egg!

Leyla was looking for her pens and pencils. She had searched everywhere.

'If you put things away, you would know where to find them again,' said her mum, taking the pencils from the box and handing them to Leyla.

'Have you seen my yo-yo, Mum?' asked Lucy, coming into the kitchen. Mum reached into a toy box and handed it to her.

'If you put it away, you would know where to find it again,' said Mum.

When it was time to do the shopping, Mum began to rush about the rooms, looking here and there, in pockets and on chairs.

'Has anyone seen my keys?' she asked. The little ones started to help, lifting cushions and opening drawers until, at last, the keys were found, hiding under a hat on the table.

The dinosaurs resisted the temptation to say anything, but Mum laughed.

'I know,' she said. 'If I put them away, I would know where to find them again!'

Doreen's neighbours were painting the outside of their house. Doreen loved painting. 'Can I help?' she asked.

'All right, if you're very careful,' said the neighbours.

They had red paint for the walls, and white paint for the window frames. Doreen went around the back of the house, away from everyone else, where she had a whole wall to herself. She painted a big umbrella, and a beach-ball, and a dinosaur in a red and white stripey swimming costume. She had a lovely time.

Then she heard a friend of the neighbours arrive, who had come to visit them. They all walked round the house, and suddenly saw the wall Doreen had been painting. The neighbours were very angry, but just as they opened their mouths to say something, their friend exclaimed, 'How clever! A sunny beach scene to look at all year round! Would you do one for me?'

The neighbours liked the idea of starting a new fashion. Suddenly, they began to smile. Doreen was very relieved, and spent the whole summer painting houses!

Come on, Tony!' called his mother. 'We're all packed up and ready to go.'

The family were off on holiday. They were going camping by the seaside, and they were taking so many things. Buckets and spades, sleeping bags, pots and pans, books and games and Tee-shirts and shorts.

'I'm not going without Steggy,' said Tony, crossly. Steggy was the toy Stegosaurus who had shared Tony's bed since he was tiny. He couldn't go to sleep without Steggy, and now he had lost him.

'We're not waiting any longer, Tony,' said his father. 'You're coming—NOW!'

So Tony came, but he wasn't happy. He grumbled and moaned all the way to the seaside. And when it was time to go to bed in their cosy tent, he just cried.

'Cheer up, Tony,' said his sister, unrolling his sleeping bag for him. And who should fall out but—Steggy!

'I remember now,' said Tony happily, 'I packed him myself, so he wouldn't be forgotten. Now I'm going to have the best holiday ever!'

Rachel had seen a poster for a circus. It showed acrobats and tightrope walkers, performing dogs and clowns.

'I'm sorry, but it's too far for us to go,' said her dad. Rachel was very disappointed, and told her friend Chuck all about it.

'Let's make our own circus, instead,' he suggested. 'We could do anything we like. I bet our friends would come to watch—and they could join in, too!' So all that afternoon they practised their acts, until they were ready with a splendid show.

Chuck did cartwheels and somersaults—forwards and backwards—and balanced on a plank of wood. Rachel danced and stood on one leg on the swing—and everyone pretended that she was very high off the ground. They bowled hoops to each other, then put on silly hats and chased around the ring. It was such a marvellous circus that the audience even joined in for the grand parade, marching round and pretending to play musical instruments. And none of them even gave a thought to the other circus—they were all having too much fun.

Jeanette and Jessica were identical twins. Both had the same green eyes, the same brown, scaly skin, the same long tails. Only dinosaurs who knew them well had learned to tell them apart. One day, Murray was boasting that he was the fastest runner in school.

'I'm fed up with him showing off,' said Jessica. 'I have an idea to teach him a lesson.'

The next day, the twins and their friends were having races in the playground. Up marched Murray.

'Slow coaches,' mocked Murray. 'I can run twice as fast as that without even trying!' Jeanette came forward while Jessica quietly walked away, unnoticed.

'Race you round the school then,' challenged Jeanette.

'I'm ready any time,' said Murray. Timmy was to be the starter. Jeanette and Murray lined up.

'On your marks, get set—go!' said Timmy, and they raced off round the school.

Murray slowly took the lead, but Jeanette was close behind as they raced past the tree where Jessica had hidden. Jeanette slipped into the hiding place, as Jessica dashed out, so full of energy that she soon overtook Murray and beat him to the finishing line. Everyone cheered the winner—and Murray never found out that he was only beaten by twin speed!

I

t's not fair,' moaned Rebecca. 'I want a day off school as well as Scott.'

'Scott has spots, a high temperature and feels poorly,' said Mum. 'You'll have more fun at school than he will at home.'

Rebecca went off to school in a bad mood. She could not concentrate on her lessons because she kept thinking about Scott at home. She imagined he was having a great time while she was hard at work. It wasn't fair! She did not know that while she was building a cardboard spaceship, listening to stories, measuring the desks, and rushing about the playground, Scott was in bed feeling hot, itchy and unhappy.

When Rebecca woke up the next morning, she felt hot and bothered. Her face was pink and blotchy and she could not eat her breakfast.

'Back to bed,' ordered Mum.

'But Mrs Bronto said we could paint pictures of our garden today and we were going on a nature walk,' wailed Rebecca, almost in tears. 'It's not fair.' Her Mum smiled kindly as she tucked her back into bed.

'This time, I agree with you,' she said. 'It's not nice feeling poorly—as I am sure Scott could have told you yesterday. It's much more fun at school.'

Jessie was a very lucky dinosaur. Her grandma owned a tea shop, and every day her mum would take her there and let her play while she helped Grandma with the sandwiches. The shop was full of delicious things, like ice-cream and sticky buns. But the things that Jessie liked best were the chocolate eclairs. One day, the telephone rang while Grandma was making the chocolate icing for the eclairs. She went off to answer it, leaving the bowl on the table. Jessie knew she would get into trouble if her grandma found her licking the bowl, so as quick as a flash, she took the whole thing and ran off into the garden. The icing was delicious! Jessie ate spoon after spoon.

Inside, she heard Grandma saying, 'I'm sure I left some icing just there. I must be going mad!'

Jessie laughed and laughed, but suddenly, she began to feel very ill . . .

Betsy's father loved gardening. He spent every weekend pulling out the weeds and trimming the lawn. He was very proud of all his work, and his was the best-kept garden in the neighbourhood. He had a big vegetable patch at the back of the garden where he grew potatoes, and rhubarb and cabbages. This year he was planning to enter some of his potato plants in the local gardening competition, and had spent more time than ever tending to them, until the plants stood even taller than Betsy!

One day, Betsy and her friend Dinah were playing in the garden. One of their favourite games was making houses, and the big potato plants looked a perfect place for a cosy little house. They walked in, pushed the big leafy plants aside, until they got right to the middle. Then they squashed all the leaves down in a round circle. It was a perfect house! It was cool and green and had a path all the way out to . . . Oops! There, at the end of the path, was Betsy's dad. And he didn't look very happy!

THE NEST

All Katie's friends seemed to have lots of brothers and sisters. Sometimes, Katie thought it was better to have her mum and dad to herself. But at other times, she wished she was part of a large brood so she always had someone to play with.

Early one spring, her mother seemed preoccupied and was often too tired to play with Katie. At other times she bustled about looking very busy, although Katie could never quite work out what she was doing. Dad was too busy decorating to spare her any time. Katie felt lonely and left out.

One day, she came home late from a walk. She had been daydreaming about belonging to a big family and had forgotten the time. She rushed into the room, her excuse ready, expecting to be told off. But her mother just rushed up to her and gave her a hug! Then she led Katie into the newly decorated room.

Katie could hardly believe her eyes. There in the corner, tucked up soft and cosy, was a nest. And inside the nest were four beautiful, green eggs.

'You are going to have some brothers and sisters soon,' said her mum proudly. 'Will you help me to care for them?'

'Oh, yes,' cried Katie. 'I'll be the best big sister ever.'

Dan was having trouble with his sums at school.

'I always get them muddled,' he said grumpily, stamping his foot, as he often did when he was cross. 'I'm not going to do any more. I don't care if I can't remember.'

His Mum knew better than to argue with him when he was feeling so cross. She watched him run down the path to his favourite thinking place—the gate at the bottom of the garden. He always sat there when he wanted to sulk, she thought to herself. Then an idea came to her, and she got out a pencil and paper and jotted down a little rhyme to help Dan with his sums.

'Pat a cake, pat a cake
Stamp on the floor
Two plus two is always four!
Pat a cake, pat a cake
Sit on the gate
Four plus four is always eight!'

And even though Dan is much bigger now, he always remembers that little rhyme.

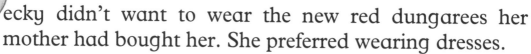

Becky didn't want to wear the new red dungarees her mother had bought her. She preferred wearing dresses.

'But you must wear them,' pleaded her mother. 'You'll look so sweet—and they're your favourite colour.'

When it was time to go to the park, Becky was still upstairs in her bedroom, dressed in her pyjamas.

'We'll go without you!' threatened her mother. Becky reluctantly put on her new dungarees.

At the park, Becky soon found she could join all the other dinosaurs climbing up the steep steps of the long slide, playing on the see-saw, and sitting in the sand-pit, without her dress getting in the way as it usually did.

'I like my new dungarees!' said Becky happily, when her mother took her home.

Time to go to the dentist,' called Charlie's dad.

'I don't want to!' shouted Charlie. He was hiding.

'If you don't go to the dentist,' said Mr Centrosaurus pulling Charlie out of his hiding place, 'you'll never grow up with big strong healthy teeth.'

'Noooo!' cried Charlie all the way to the dentist.

'Waaaaah!' he wailed in the dentist's waiting-room.

'What bad manners,' whispered a lady patient.

Charlie's dad let go of him. Charlie ran through a door and found himself in a big white room. In the middle of the room was a shiny silver chair with levers on it. Charlie sat in the chair and pulled some of the levers. The chair whizzed up and down.

'Are you Charlie?' said a voice. 'What lovely teeth. Can I see them?' It was a lady in a white coat.

'All right,' said Charlie. 'I've just escaped from the dentist,' he added proudly.

The lady whizzed him up on the chair and looked at his teeth with a little mirror. Then she polished them with a special electric brush.

'All done,' she said. 'That wasn't so bad, was it?'

'No,' said Charlie. 'That was fun!'

Then Charlie's dad appeared at the door and Charlie realized . . . he had been at the dentist's all along!

I'm not scared of anything!' boasted Susie Stegosaurus.

'Well I bet you don't dare go into the haunted house,' sneered her brother, James.

'Bet you don't, either,' said Susie.

'Bet I do, too,' said James. 'Let's go right now.'

Susie and James sneaked up the overgrown path and pushed open the creaky door.

'I'm not s-scared,' shivered Susie.

'M-me neither,' trembled James.

They crept up the winding stairs.

'Bet you're f-frightened,' stammered James.

'I'm n-no scaredycat,' stuttered Susie.

They opened the door of the dark, cobwebby room and tiptoed in.

'W-well,' whispered Susie, 'I suppose neither of us are scaredycats.'

'I s-suppose not,' whispered James.

'Eeeeek!' squeaked a mouse.

'Arrrghhh!' screamed James.

'Help!' shrieked Susie.

And they both ran out of the cobwebby room and down the winding stairs, through the creaky door and up the overgrown path, all the way back home to bed.

Just as Owen and his mum came home from shopping, the doorbell rang.

'I wanted to catch you before you took off your coat,' Mrs Dimetrodon said as they opened the door.

'Do tell me the name of these lovely blue flowers.'

'I won't be long, Owen,' Mum sighed as she was led next door. Suddenly, a gust of wind blew the door closed with a bang.

'Oh!' cried Mum. 'My keys are in the house. Owen,' she called. 'Can you open the door?' But Owen was too small to reach the latch.

'Get a chair,' said Mum. But the latch was too stiff for Owen's small hands.

'I'm locked in,' wailed Owen. 'I want my mum!'

'What shall we do?' muttered the little crowd which was by now spreading down the path.

Mum pulled out a hanky to blow her nose, for she was beginning to feel rather upset. There was a loud jingle in her pocket and all the chattering stopped.

'Oh dear!' said Mum, holding up the keys and blushing. 'They must have been there all the time.'

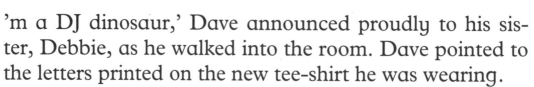

I'm a DJ dinosaur,' Dave announced proudly to his sister, Debbie, as he walked into the room. Dave pointed to the letters printed on the new tee-shirt he was wearing.

'What does that mean?' asked Debbie, who was much more interested in a colourful box she had bought.

'Disc jockey!' replied Dave. 'My friend, Mike, has asked me to pick and play the music at his party tomorrow. His mum even gave me this special tee-shirt from the clothes store she owns.'

While Dave sorted through his collection of pop tapes, Debbie placed her box on the table. When Dave turned round, she asked him to open it.

As her brother lifted the lid, a funny toy-insect sprang out and squeaked loudly. It made Dave jump!

'I bought that from the joke shop!' giggled Debbie.

'I'm going to ask Mike if his mum has another 'DJ' tee-shirt for you,' Dave laughed.

'Why? I'm not a disc jockey,' said his sister.

'No,' grinned Dave. 'You're *Debbie* the *Joker*!'

Dad was going to take Billy and his friend Trevor to the park, but first they had to tidy up the house. Billy helped Dad to wash up.

'No, Billy. Not like that—like this,' said his father, rinsing all the foam off the dishes.

Then there were lots of Billy's clothes to put away.

'No, Billy. Not like that—like this,' said Dad, folding them up neatly.

Then all the toys had to be cleared away.

'No, Billy. Not like that—like this,' said Dad, finding the right box for each one.

At last it was time to go. When they got to the park, Dad started to play football. He was hopeless!

'No, Dad. Not like that—like this,' said Billy kicking the ball into goal. Then Trevor got his skateboard out. Dad wanted a go.

'No, not like that—like this,' said Trevor showing him how to balance.

Then they played tag. Billy caught Dad every time.

'Your dad's not much good at playing,' said Trevor.

'I know,' said Billy. 'But he's learning.'

O h, Mum!' wailed Jack, looking out of the window. 'It's raining hadrosaurs and stegosaurs!'

Jack's friend Catherine was coming to play, and Mum had promised them a picnic in the park. But how could they have a picnic in the pouring rain?

'Never mind,' said Mum. 'I've got an idea.' She took a big tablecloth out of the cupboard and went into the kitchen, shutting the door behind her.

When Catherine arrived, she and Jack played cards for a while. When Mum called out, 'Time to eat!' they raced into the kitchen.

In the middle of the floor was their very own dinosaur den, with the table for a roof and the tablecloth for walls—and the picnic was ready and waiting for them inside! Mum had piled rocks all around, and there was a big notice pinned to the cloth that said 'Jack and Catherine's cave—keep out!'

'Oh, Mum,' said Jack, 'this is brilliant! Can we always have our picnics inside?'

ROCKY GETS LOST!

John had a very tiny dinosaur friend. He was called Rocky. Rocky was a little shy, and spent a lot of his time sleeping. He liked nothing better than to curl up in John's mum's warm ironing basket, on top of all the clothes.

One day, John lost Rocky. He looked in the ironing basket, but there was nothing there. He looked all over his room, under the bed and behind the bookcase. He even looked in the rock garden outside, where Rocky liked to play at being a big ferocious dinosaur in amongst the plants and stones. But Rocky wasn't there either. Just then, John heard some tiny squeaking noises that seemed to be coming from his chest of drawers. Then he heard the noise again. He walked up to the top drawer very carefully, and opened it quickly. There was Rocky, looking rumpled and a bit annoyed! He had fallen asleep in the ironing, and been put away in the drawer along with the rest of the clothes. Poor Rocky! John was very pleased to have found him again.

Your cousin Lorraine's coming to stay next week,' Mum said to Sarah. 'That'll be nice, won't it?'

'No,' said Sarah. She remembered when Lorraine had come to stay last year. She'd brought lots of dolls and all she did was sit inside and play with them. She always looked neat and tidy, and everyone said, 'What a good little dinosaur Lorraine is!'

But Lorraine was different this time. She didn't bring any dolls with her—she brought a scooter. And she certainly didn't look neat and tidy!

On Monday, Lorraine made a den out of chairs and a rug in the sitting-room.

On Tuesday, Lorraine dug up all the flowers in the garden to make a big bonfire.

On Wednesday, Lorraine crashed her scooter into Mrs Iguanadon's fence.

On Thursday, Lorraine made a very strange cake—using all the food in the cupboard.

On Friday, Lorraine and Sarah had a midnight feast.

On Saturday, it was time for Lorraine to go home.

'Can Cousin Lorraine come and stay again soon?' asked Sarah.

'No,' said her mother. 'Let's have a rest from Lorraine for a while.'

Charlie loved bicycles. Every day, on the way to school, he would stop and gaze in the window of the bicycle shop. There were all sorts of bicycles, but Charlie liked one special shiny red one. He asked his parents if they would buy it for him, but they just said, 'Don't be silly. You can't even *ride* a bicycle!'

Charlie's friend Gary was an acrobat in the circus, and was very good at balancing on things. 'Would you help me learn to ride a bicycle?' Charlie asked.

Gary helped Charlie practise. It was very difficult and Charlie kept falling off. But eventually he could stay on with Gary holding him. Finally, Gary let go! Charlie wobbled a bit, but rode all the way home with Gary running along behind. His parents were amazed to see him riding up the driveway all by himself!

The next morning, when Charlie opened his eyes, he saw a beautiful red shiny bicycle right next to his bed!

THE BIRTHDAY PRESENT

William and Joanna were in a fix. Mum's birthday was in two days but they could not think of anything nice that they could afford to buy. Dad was not much help.

'She won't expect you to buy a present,' he said. 'Why not paint her a picture instead?' But they wanted to buy her a present. So they sat in their thinking spot in the garden and vowed to stay there until they had a plan. It took until tea time before William hit on an idea.

The next day, they returned from the shops, hiding a brown paper bag behind their backs. Paper and paints were sneaked into their bedroom where laughter could be heard through the closed door.

The next morning, Mum was woken at just the right time with a cup of tea, a beautifully painted birthday card and a chorus of 'Happy Birthday!'

'Thank you,' replied Mum, admiring the colourful flowers on the card. 'Is that me wearing the knitted hat? It suits me. And the flowers are lovely.'

'Oh, good,' the little dinosaurs replied, handing her a brown paper parcel painted with flowers. Mum opened it to reveal a packet of seeds and some wool. 'We bought you the seeds and the wool, and the pictures are to show what they will look like when you have grown the flowers and knitted the hat.'

'What a lovely idea,' said Mum.

THE WISHING POOL

One sunny day, a young dinosaur called Morris was sitting beside a pool, dreaming about this and that and watching the other dinosaurs in the forest.

'I wish I had three fine horns like Triceratops,' he thought to himself. At once, he felt a strange tingling in his head. And when he looked at himself in the still water, there were the horns!

'This must be a wishing pool!' thought Morris. And in no time at all he had wished for wings like Pteranodon, a long neck like Diplodocus and teeth like Tyrannosaurus Rex.

'Help! It's a monster!' screamed his mother when Morris came home for tea, flapping his wings, stretching his neck and baring his teeth.

'Go away!' shouted Morris's friends when he tried to play with them.

'Grrrr!' growled the great Tyrannosaurus when he saw Morris's sharp teeth.

Morris went straight back to the pool and wished as hard as he could to be ordinary Morris. After that, he never tried wishing again!

BABIES ARE BORING

Terry and Rex were on their way to see Auntie Dinah and her new baby. They were very excited at the thought of a new playmate.

'Where is it?' cried Terry when they arrived.

'There,' said Auntie Dinah, pointing to a smooth shiny object in the corner. 'It's in the egg.'

It didn't move or smile or play. 'Babies are boring,' said Terry and went out to play.

Rex was doing his homework when he heard a sound. 'CRACK' it went, and 'CRACK' again, and then, 'CRACK'. Rex saw a little hole appear in the egg. It got bigger and bigger. Out popped a head and then a body. And there, looking curiously at them, was the cutest little dinosaur in the world.

'Terry, Terry! Come and see!' yelled Rex.

Terry rushed in. 'Oh Gee!' he said. 'Babies aren't boring after all!'

SEEKING SHADE

It was a fine day so Big Dinosaur and Little Dinosaur put on their sunhats and took a picnic to the beach.

'Perhaps we should have gone to the park instead,' said Little Dinosaur shortly after they arrived.

'Why?' asked Big Dinosaur.

'There are lots of shady trees to sit under,' replied Little Dinosaur. 'I'm getting hot!'

Big Dinosaur went to the beach café to hire a large umbrella but they were all being used.

'One's due to be returned very soon,' said the café owner. 'Then you can have it.'

'What shall we do till then?' asked Little Dinosaur when he heard.

'I'll show you some shade,' grinned Big Dinosaur.

Little Dinosaur was puzzled. He looked up and down the beach. All he could see was sand. 'Where?' he asked.

Big Dinosaur lay on his towel and pulled the sunhat over his eyes. Little Dinosaur laughed. 'Now I see the shade!' he said. 'I can sit in your huge *shadow*!'

Karl's dad took him to a fairground. But, try as he might, Karl could not win a prize at the Hoop-la stall.

'Watch me, son,' grinned Dad.

Taking aim, he tossed a hoop over a jar of cookies and won them! On the way home, Karl thoughtfully munched a cookie. 'I really enjoyed myself. Thanks, Dad,' he said. 'I wish I could throw a hoop like you did!'

'It just takes practice,' Dad replied. 'I'll help you, if you like.'

Karl eagerly agreed, so his dad found some small rubber rings in the garage. Then he called Karl.

'All you have to do is throw the rings at me,' said Dad. Karl was puzzled.

'How will playing catch help?' he asked.

His dad chuckled. 'Not catch, silly. Hoop-la! You have to throw the hoops over my horns.'

Karl carefully began to toss the rings over the three horns on his dad's head. Soon he could do it with ease. And next day, when they returned to the Hoop-la stall, who do you think won a prize? Karl, of course!

Mr Diplodocus was a very stylish dresser. There wasn't a single day that he wasn't well turned out, all the long way from his top hat to his shiny shoes.

But what Mr Diplodocus wanted more than anything else, was a bow-tie. Luckily, it was his birthday in one week's time, so it was a perfect opportunity to tell all his friends what he wanted. And that is exactly what he did.

On his birthday, Mr Diplodocus had *piles* of presents. He unwrapped the first present, and was delighted to find a pink and blue striped bow-tie. 'Wonderful!' he exclaimed, and went on to unwrap the second gift. 'Another bow-tie!' he cried. And so it went on. Every single parcel contained a colourful bow-tie.

Luckily for Mr Diplodocus, he didn't have to upset any of his friends by only wearing one of his presents — he had such a long neck that he could wear every single one. What a spectacular sight Mr Diplodocus made, as he walked proudly down the street wearing no less than twenty bow-ties!

Sam loved chocolate more than anything else.

'One of these days you'll turn into chocolate,' his mum warned. That night, Sam sat in bed reading a book about a chocolate tree. Soon he fell asleep.

Sam could see the chocolate tree in front of him as he walked through the forest. As he got nearer, he thought he could make out a gnarled face in the folds of the bark. Suddenly, a broad smile spread across the tree and two beady eyes popped open.

'Hello,' said a deep, chocolatey voice. 'Do take a bite.' Sam picked off a few leaves. They melted on his tongue. He couldn't resist just another bite—or two, or three. Then his hands felt sticky. He tried to wipe them clean on his handkerchief, but to his dismay, he found that he could not wipe the chocolate off his fingers, for his fingers *were* chocolate—and his arms, and his legs!

'But I don't want to be chocolate!' he cried out.

'I was only joking, dear,' said his mum. 'You won't turn into chocolate.' Sam opened his eyes.

'I do like chocolate, Mum,' he said. 'But I think I'll eat less of it from now on.'

Ben was bored. He'd been playing by himself all morning and now he'd run out of things to do.

'Come outside,' called his mother. 'It's a lovely spring day and you can help me with the gardening.'

'Gardening's boring,' said Ben.

'No, it's not,' said his mother. 'Look, you can have this patch of earth and make a garden all of your own.'

'All right,' said Ben. He found the shells he'd picked up on the beach last summer and put them all round the edge. His mother gave him some seeds and he dug a tiny hole for each one with a teaspoon, popped it in and covered it up with earth. He sprayed the seeds with water so that they would grow.

Then one fine summer's day, Ben was running down the path when he saw a jungle of nasturtiums, cornflowers and marigolds.

'Look, I grew these flowers,' said Ben to his mother. 'Gardening's great!'

THE SPELLING TEST

Terence Pterodactyl was an extremely clever little dinosaur. At school he came top in every subject. There was nothing that Terence Pterodactyl couldn't do.

One day, his teacher announced to the class that she was going to give them a spelling test. All Terence's friends were very worried about it. But not Terence—he could spell anything, no trouble at all.

At the spelling test, the teacher said, 'Emma—spell JURASSIC.'

'J-E-R-A-S-S-I-K' said Emma, nervously,

'That's wrong,' said the teacher. 'Terence—*you* try.'

'J-U-R-A-S-S-I-C' he quickly replied.

'Well done, Terence. You *are* clever,' said the teacher. 'Now spell PTERODACTYL.'

'Easy!' he sneered. But try as he might, Terence couldn't get it right. The word *seemed* to begin with a 'T', it *sounded* like a 'T', and yet every time he started off with 'T', the teacher shouted 'Wrong!' Poor Terence didn't know it started with a 'P'.

His friends suddenly felt much better—Terence, the dinosaur who could do anything, couldn't spell his own name! 'Never mind, Terry,' they said, after school. 'At least you know what it feels like to be wrong!'

aisy had a sunshade which she carried everywhere. Sunny or cloudy, whatever the weather, she never left it behind. One dull day, Daisy walked around the garden happily twirling the sunshade over her head.

'Why carry that silly sunshade when the sun isn't shining?' teased her brother, Brad. 'I'm off next door, to play marbles with Mark. Want to join us?'

Daisy shook her head. She wanted to play with her sunshade. She was still in the garden when her mum called, 'Lunch time! Go and fetch Brad, please!'

Mark and Brad were putting away their marbles. Suddenly, her brother's bag split. All the marbles dropped out and rolled across the floor.

'How will I get them home?' said Brad as he began to pick them up.

'Easy,' smiled Daisy. Opening her sunshade, she held it upside-down like a basket and put the marbles into it.

'Sunshades aren't so silly!' admitted Brad. 'Shall *I* carry it home for you, Daisy?'

THE GARDEN SHED

It was the day before Ellen's birthday, but she was afraid everyone had forgotten. All her family seemed interested in was the garden shed. Ellen's sister Susan had two pots of pink paint (Ellen's favourite colour).

'I'm going to paint the shed.' said Susan, 'so it will look smart this summer.'

When Ellen's mum came in that evening, she had a big bag of ribbons and silver paper.

'I'm going to decorate the shed.' said Ellen's mum, 'so it will look cheerful this summer.'

Grandpa was hiding something behind his back.

'I'm putting these cushions in the shed,' he said, 'so we can sit there when it's warm.'

Ellen's brother, Tom, had some lemonade and cakes.

'I suppose they're for the shed too,' sighed Ellen.

'Yes,' he said, 'I'm going to store them in there.'

On Ellen's birthday there were no cards, no decorations and no cake. They *had* forgotten.

'Come and see the shed, Ellen,' said her family.

When Ellen opened the shed door her family shouted 'SURPRISE!' The shed was painted pink with HAPPY BIRTHDAY ELLEN on the wall in silver paper, and on the table were cards, presents and a great big birthday cake. They *had* remembered after all.

Naomi was a very pretty dinosaur with beautiful, crinkly, green skin and a cute little horn on her pointed snout. The trouble was that Naomi was proud of being pretty, and she let everyone know it!

One day, the class were taking a boat trip. They set off in a neat line of pairs, but Naomi walked alone.

'None of you is good-looking enough to walk with me,' she said, lifting her snout higher into the air.

With their coats buttoned tight and the wind on their scales, they pointed over stern and bow, chattering incessantly, as the Captain pointed out the sights. Naomi sat alone, not happy at being ignored.

Suddenly, it began to rain, and all the dinosaurs rushed pell-mell towards the cabin. All except Naomi, who ambled after them, snout so high that she did not see the rope across the deck and fell headlong into a puddle. The children laughed when they saw her bedraggled pink bow and muddy face. For once, Naomi was not happy to be the centre of attention.

'No one likes me,' she wailed to Mrs Skeggs.

'Why not try liking them?' suggested Mrs Skeggs. 'Then perhaps they will like you, too.'

Naomi dried her tears, straightened her bow and smiled. 'I'll try,' she said. And she did.

Right on time!' grinned Mr Docus as Mark opened the gate and hurried up the path to the front door with the 'Dinosaur News'. Mark always arrived at five o'clock each afternoon, on his paper round.

Next morning, a cement-mixer rumbled in Mr Docus's front garden as he set to work to lay a new path.

He finished just minutes before Mark was due with the newspaper. Mr Docus went indoors and wrote 'WET CEMENT' on some card to tie to the gate.

Mrs Docus peered from the window at the cement path. 'It's very plain,' she said. 'It needs a pattern.'

'What sort?' asked Mr Docus, thinking hard. He forgot about Mark who came racing up the path as usual, leaving a perfect trail of footprints behind him.

'I'm sorry!' he said when he saw what he had done.

'Don't be,' laughed Mr Docus. 'It's the perfect pattern!'

'And most unusual,' Mrs Docus agreed.

Emma was a shy dinosaur. She loved to play with dolls and read books. She had lots of friends, but what she wanted most of all was a special friend of her own.

One day, their teacher introduced them to Sally, who was joining the class. Hands shot into the air.

'Can I look after her?' 'Oh, me!' cried the children. But Emma was too shy to put up her hand.

Kitty and Michael were chosen, and for the first week, they showed Sally where everything was kept and played with her at playtime and lunchtime. Emma just watched. She very much wanted to be Sally's friend, too, but she was too shy to say anything.

Sally soon settled into the class and Kitty and Michael began to play with their old friends again. One playtime, Sally was reading as Emma walked past.

'That's my favourite book,' said Emma shyly.

'Really?' said Sally. 'It's my favourite, too. I love the bit when the bad dinosaur falls into the river and they fish him out in a net! That's funny!'

'I laugh at that, too,' said Emma, and they chatted on until it was time for lessons.

After that, Sally and Emma always sat together in class, played together at playtime, and read together at reading time. And Emma did not feel so shy now that she had a special friend of her own.

THE EGG AND SPOON RACE

Walter and his friends were going in for the egg and spoon race at their school sports day. They had to run along, balancing an egg on a spoon, and the first person over the finishing line would win. Now, they were practising.

Lucy held her egg straight out in front of her and ran with tiny little steps.

George carried his egg close against his chest and took great big strides.

Donna held her egg on the spoon with her thumb and raced as fast as she could.

But Walter just walked along very carefully, making sure his egg didn't fall.

'Walter's going to be last!' laughed his friends. Walter ignored them.

'On your marks, get set, go!' shouted their teacher, and the race began.

Lucy didn't look where she was going and ran around in circles.

George's egg fell off his spoon and rolled into a hole.

Donna was sent home by the teacher for cheating.

And where was Walter? Walking along very carefully — first over the finishing line!

Madeleine and Isobel wanted to play in a band. They would make the instruments, learn the tunes and put on a show. There was plenty of time—it was an hour until tea-time.

Isobel borrowed a wooden spoon, an old saucepan and two saucepan lids from her mum. Madeleine found an empty shoe box, some elastic bands and a whistle from a Christmas cracker. This was going to be easy!

The garden rug was soon spread across the grass, and the drum and cymbals placed in the middle.

Madeleine stretched the elastic bands round the shoe box, and then twanged them to test the sound.

'Just like a real guitar,' she beamed. 'And I'll keep the whistle in my top pocket so it's handy.'

'Let's not practise,' said Madeleine. 'I'm sure we'll be fine.' So they went to fetch the audience: Isobel's Mum, Auntie Millie and baby brother, Tom.

The concert was a resounding success. Tom yelled at the first song, but once they let him bang the drum, he joined in happily, and it didn't matter that he wasn't quite in time with the music. The audience said they could not wait to hear the next show—and Isobel and Madeleine couldn't wait to perform!

Peter and Leo were the best of friends. They lived close to each other, they played together and they sometimes stayed the night at each other's houses.

One day, though, they had a fight. It started off as a game, but Peter squeezed Leo a little too tightly and Leo butted Peter rather too hard, and before they knew it they were really hurting each other.

After that, they stopped playing together and they didn't even smile if they passed each other by. Peter felt very lonely and Leo missed Peter too, but they didn't know how to make up.

Then one afternoon Leo was coming back from school and he saw Peter with three bigger dinosaurs. They were pulling his tail and Peter was crying.

'Leave him alone!' shouted Leo. 'He's my friend.'

The other dinosaurs ran off, and Peter and Leo went home together.

'I'm glad we're still friends,' said Peter. 'Let's not fight ever again.'

Once upon a time, there was a dinosaur who set out to travel the world in search of adventure.

So off she went, to see what there was to be seen. She climbed up great high mountains, covered in pine trees. She slithered down steep gorges and swam in icy lakes, crossed deserts and splashed though muddy swamps.

And what amazing creatures she came across! Huge dinosaurs with legs like tree trunks that made the earth shake when they stamped along; flying dinosaurs whose scaly wings made the air rush and swirl as they soared through the sky; swimming dinosaurs who whipped the water into a froth with their enormous fins.

Then one day, she decided it was time to go home.

'Tell us what there is in the world,' said the other dinosaurs when she got back. And every night they would curl up by the fire and listen to stories of amazing adventures that made their spines prickle. But they never dared go travelling themselves.

Christopher had waited ages for the day when his family were to move house. He had asked his mum every day, 'Is it today, Mum? Can we move today?'

Now at last Christopher stood in his room, surrounded by boxes. He could hardly wait! Soon he would be in his new home.

'I'll have a last look to make sure we haven't left anything,' said Mum. Christopher went with her.

'Nothing here . . . nothing there . . .' muttered his Mum as she scurried from room to room.

Christopher peered into his empty room. A toy dinosaur lay abandoned on the floor. He picked it up. This was *his* room—nowhere else could be the same!

'Mum,' he wailed, the tears rising, 'I don't want to move!' His mum rushed to comfort him, but he spent an unhappy journey to the new house.

He picked up the smallest box and followed his parents to a large, sunny room with a big window. There was a cupboard in the corner which was just right for his toys, and a neat alcove for his bed.

'My bed can go here, my desk there,' he grinned. 'It's not the same as my old room—it's better!'

Oh, it will be splendid!' cried Esther. 'Can we really look after cousin Bertie for the whole day?'

'Yes,' replied Mum, 'and you'll have to help us, Eric. Looking after a baby is hard work.' Eric groaned.

Auntie and Uncle delivered the smiling baby. As the door closed behind them, Bertie howled.

'Come for a cuddle,' suggested Esther. 'Would you like a biscuit? Are you thirsty?' Still Bertie yelled. Eric had had enough already. He thumped his fist on the table.

"Oh, please,' he moaned. "Do we have to put up with this all day?' There was silence! Bertie looked at him then banged his little fist on the table.

'Oplzz,' he mimicked, 'aweggupalay!'

They played parrots and Bertie copied everything that Esther and Eric said or did. They banged saucepan lids until Mum couldn't stand it any longer. They built towers of bricks for Bertie to knock down and brought him rattles to shake. They fed the ducks at the park and swung on the swings.

By the time his parents returned, Bertie was fed, bathed and in his pyjamas. He was fast asleep. But they had to knock loudly on the door because Mum, Esther and Eric had all fallen asleep as well!

Arnie was a magic dinosaur. If he concentrated very hard on anything, he could change his shape and colour, so that he looked like a tree, or a traffic light, or his Great Aunt Jane, who was very ugly (this was his friends' favourite one). But Arnie wasn't very good at controlling his magic talent. Sometimes, when he was watching the sports on television, he would suddenly turn into a football, which always made his mum and dad drop their dinner in surprise! Other times, no matter what he did, he was just plain Arnie.

One day, on the way home from school, Arnie saw some nasty-looking men with guns and sacks stealing money from the bank. This was his big chance! He concentrated harder than ever before, and tried and tried until . . . he made himself look like Percy the Policeman! The robbers ran off in fright. Arnie got a huge reward for his magic trick, and went to a beach with all his family, where he happily concentrated on being a surfboard for two whole weeks!

Jane and her little brother Ricky had gone to Hayley's house. Hayley and Jane were playing, but whenever Ricky tried to join in, the girls said, 'You can't play — you're too little. Go away!'

Ricky was too little to draw pictures, he was too little to go in the wendy house, and he was too little to dress up. So instead, he started to play with a ball.

He could hear Hayley's baby sister crying, but when she saw Ricky chasing the ball, she stopped.

Ricky rolled the ball across the floor and the baby rolled it back. She smiled at him.

Ricky bounced the ball and threw it up in the air with the end of his tail. The baby started to laugh.

Hayley's mother brought Ricky and the baby some juice and biscuits. After that, she gave Ricky a tricycle that Hayley had grown out of. Ricky rode in circles round the baby, and she laughed and laughed.

When Jane and Hayley came in, they wanted to ride the tricycle. But Ricky said, 'You're too big. Go away!'

It was a bitterly cold winter. Maria could not remember when it had been so cold.

'Nonsense,' said Grandpa. 'It was colder when I was young. Once it was so cold that the lake froze, and we went skating on the ice.' Maria hoped it would get that cold and she could go skating. But Grandpa always said things were better when he was young.

Each day when Grandpa returned from his walk, brushing off snow and stamping his feet, he would say, 'It's not as cold as when I was a lad.' For two weeks this went on, until Maria decided she would never be able to ice-skate. When Grandpa came in that day, she could hardly believe what she heard.

'It's even colder than when I was a lad!'

'What was that, Grandpa?' she asked.

'You heard!' laughed Grandpa. 'The ice is so thick, it is safe for the heaviest dinosaur. Let's go skating!'

What a wonderful time they had. Maria fell over many times before she got the knack, but soon they were zooming this way and that.

'That was wonderful, Grandpa,' said Maria.

'It was, wasn't it?' replied Grandpa with a smile. 'It was even better than when I was young!'

Kirsty and Callum had known Gemma ever since they hatched. They used to play together every week. When Gemma's family moved away, the children had been very sad. Now Gemma and her mother were coming to visit, and Kirsty and Callum were worried.

'What if we don't know what to play any more?' asked Callum, anxiously.

'I don't think we'll like each other now that we're older,' said Kirsty.

'I am sure you will get on just fine when you meet again,' they were told.

Gemma bounced with excitement in the back of the car, despite her fears. Kirsty and Callum paced up and down impatiently.

'When is she coming? Is it time? Are you sure she'll like us?' they had been asking all morning.

Then — knock knock! Here they were at last — smiling faces, hugs and kisses, cups of tea and home-made biscuits. But where were the children? They had disappeared less than a minute after they had arrived.

Their mums peered round Kirsty's bedroom door. Tea things were set out on a cloth, teddies were arranged in neat rows around the edge, and the dinosaurs were chattering away about this and that and five dozen other things as if they had never been apart.

Rich and Andy went to the park to play football. It was very warm so they took off their sweaters and marked out a goal with them.

'You be goalkeeper first, Rich,' said Andy.

Then he took a flying kick at the ball. BAM! It sped past Rich before he could spot it.

'Goal!' shouted Andy excitedly.

'BAM!' He soon had another goal, and another. Then Andy offered to be the goalkeeper. 'Now see how many goals you can get, Rich,' he said.

Rich placed the ball a short distance in front of the goal. Taking careful aim, he kicked it hard. But the ball missed the goal and landed in a litter-bin.

'Have another go!' said Andy.

Rich did, but the ball went wide again. However much he tried, Rich could not score a single goal.

'I'm not very good at football!' he sighed. Then he had an idea. Instead of kicking the ball, he swiped it with his powerful tail. The ball flew past Andy.

'Hurray! Goal! It's easier if dinosaurs play *tail*ball!' laughed Rich.

David had new shoes. They were very smart: blue with red laces. But there was one problem — they squeaked.

As they walked to school, David tried skipping, hopping, walking slowly and quickly. Still the shoes squeaked. The postman riding past frowned as he heard the noise and stopped to look at his bicycle.

'It's not your bike,' laughed David's mum. 'It's my son's shoes!' David blushed pink.

They passed a lady with a pram. When she heard the squeak she looked quizzically at the pram's wheels.

'It's not your pram,' said David's mum. 'It's my son's shoes!' David blushed red.

Later that morning, David was giving out the books while his teacher wrote on the blackboard.

'I hate squeaky chalk, don't you?' she said.

'It's not the chalk,' muttered David. 'It's my shoes.' At that moment the headmistress walked in. Suddenly she went pale and jumped on a chair with a squeal!

'Oh no! A mouse!' she cried. David smiled his first smile of the day.

'Don't worry, Miss,' he said. 'It's not a mouse — it's my new shoes!'

Captain Cutlass stood on deck surrounded by his crew.

'Stick with me, lads!' he cried, 'We'll be the richest and the bravest pirates sailing the seas. We sail west for seven days to dig for treasure.'

'We are with you, Captain!' they chorused.

But after seven storm-tossed days there was still no sign of land! The eighth day passed, and they ran out of food. The ninth day passed, and they ran out of water.

'Land ahoy!' shouted the bosun. Filled with new strength, they pulled on the oars, then leapt to shore. The Captain drew out the precious map which had never left his side. Glancing at his compass, he led them beyond the woodland, past Skull Mountain and over the stream to the three lonely trees.

'This is where we'll find the treasure,' he said.

The crew needed no second bidding. In minutes they were knee deep in a vast hole. Then their metal spades clanked against metal! They prised the great chest from the clinging sand, their eyes gleaming. The Captain's first blow buckled the metal. With the second, the shattered padlock gave way. He lifted the creaking lid. The treasure was theirs at last!

'Well, boys,' said Dad. 'I'm glad you found the lunch box again. Tidy up your toys now, its time to go home. What a lovely day we've had on the beach!'

Renu was a very small dinosaur who was always being bullied. She decided to invent an invisible friend who would protect her. She called him Leonard.

One day, Big Tracy invited Renu to tea. Renu knew that Big Tracy was very greedy, and that she usually left nothing for anyone else to eat. So as soon as Renu arrived, she said, 'This is my friend, Leonard. He's a cave monster. You can't see him because he is invisible, but he is VERY large and VERY fierce.'

Big Tracy looked scared. 'Don't worry,' said Renu. 'Invisible cave monsters are always good when they've had some chocolate cake.'

Big Tracy quickly cut a huge slice of chocolate cake for him. Renu pretended to feed it to Leonard, but when Big Tracy wasn't looking, she gobbled it up herself.

'Leonard is growling,' said Renu. 'I think he's still hungry. It takes a lot to fill him up.'

Big Tracy gave Leonard four more cakes, nine rock buns, and six glasses of lemonade. Renu was really feeling very full!

At five o'clock Renu and Leonard politely said good-bye. 'Thank you, Tracy,' Renu smiled. 'Leonard *is* fierce but invisible cave monsters are always good if you invite them again.'